# It Happened One Christmas

## ZEE IRWIN

USA TODAY BESTSELLING AUTHOR

# IT HAPPENED ONE CHRISTMAS

A GRUMPY & SUNSHINE, CITY VS. COUNTRY,
BILLIONAIRE CHRISTMAS ROMANCE

PART OF THE IT HAPPENED SERIES OF BOOKS

## ZEE IRWIN

CER CREATIVE COMPANY PUBLISHING

*To my mother, who has the patience of a saint.*

# CONTENTS

# CONTENT WARNINGS

Dear Readers:

I don't often feel the need to include warnings in my stories, but this particular set of characters grapple with some real-life issues. While I touch on these things lightly, I hope I told their stories with all the grace and dignity they deserved. You'll read about:

Death of a loved one due to cancer

Physical/emotional reactions to choking on food

Panic attack

Thank you for reading.

# 1

## THE BLACK BOX

### REX BUCHANAN

*T*his was it. The moment I'd been looking forward to ever since the board forced me, well, asked me to take over as CEO of Buchanan Energy thanks to my brother, Richard's, meltdown, breakdown, or whatever he wanted to call it.

I pushed through the conference room door at the Bellamy Brothers Architecture firm and barely noticed my buddy Brooks and his twin Archer before my eyes landed on the 3D model on the table. "There it is," I quickly took in the overall impression. "Stunning, at first glance," I said appreciatively, almost gushing.

"Hey, Rex. Thanks for coming today. We hoped you'd like it," Brooks greeted me.

I wasn't usually a gusher, but damn, I'd been working hard to make this project happen and finally it was within reach. The model sat on a marble slab and I read the silver plaque attached. "Rendering of the new lobby for the Buchanan Building."

"Should we give you the grand tour?" Archer asked, gloating over the design as he picked up a laser pointer.

"By all means." I rubbed my hands together while the three of us crowded the table.

Brooks took over, always the showman, the twin out front working with the clients, while Archer was more of a behind-the-scenes type of guy, engineering some of New York's top redesigns in modern skyscrapers today.

"Welcome to the new Buchanan Building. As you enter through a glass sphere here," he paused while Archer pointed the laser toward the fresh addition we would put at the front of the building my father had built back in the 70s.

"A living greenery wall will welcome visitors and workers alike to the modern era. Gone will be the days of the dark lobby with tired brown tile, tan walls, and brass fixtures. Instead, an airy space filled with light, and furnished with a minimalist white and gray palette will shine," Brooks finished his spiel.

My pants just grew tighter. Couldn't help it. This was what I lived for. Buying up New York real estate and remodeling, reselling or leasing for a profit was my passion. Not sitting behind a desk on the fortieth floor trying to run an energy company I couldn't care less about.

We had a deal, Richard and I. He was the one fascinated by the company our father, Patrick Buchanan, had built, and was happy to take over the helm. Sure, we came from old money made from decades in gas and oil, but after Dad passed away, Rich successfully ushered in a new era for the company, with a focus on clean energy.

After he stepped down and I took over the leadership of the company, I decided to do what I did best. I implemented plans to bring in a new look to the company headquarters. I could imagine Patrick in his grave, smiling at me. He was always proud of my gains and achievements among the city's elite real estate circles.

Mom, on the other hand, was still a force to be reckoned

with. But I was positive when she saw this she'd be on board with my plans to modernize Dad's building.

"Over here," Brooks continued. "You'll see the new shops and eateries planned, turning the old lobby into a multi-use space."

Archer's laser jumped from place to place as he listed off the names of the establishments who had already committed as tenants. But he glossed over one space on the corner that seemed out of place. A black box marred the white facade of my beautiful model.

"Wait, what's over there?" I pointed.

"Ah, yes. That's the existing Sun-Up Deli. Now over here—"

"What do you mean? I was told all the current tenants on the lobby floor are supposed to have been given an eviction notice. There shouldn't be a deli in the new plans."

"It seems when we consulted with your building management, there's an issue with the lease agreement for the deli." Archer pushed his glasses up the bridge of his nose. They're one way I could tell the two brothers apart. The other way was that Archer liked to dress in 3-piece suits, while Brooks was business casual.

"What issue?" I scowled. Call me spoiled, but when I wanted something, I expected it all to be smooth sailing.

"They have one of the most favorable lease agreements I've ever seen." Brooks shook his head. As a partner in some of my projects, it was familiar territory for him to handle details. "Your father and Mr. Doug Calhoun signed it twenty years ago."

"Aw hell. I remember Doug, one of my father's old cronies. He's still around?"

"Yep. Get this. He pays the original monthly lease amount; there hasn't been a single increase all this time. And, he has until midnight on New Year's Eve to either renew the lease or give notice that he intends to vacate. There's no eviction clause; you're stuck."

"What the—That's crazy. Who would make a deal like that?" My father, of course. He often took care of his friends and their families, even going so far as to put several kids through college. Sure, he was tough in business, but had a heart of gold, too. Everyone revered him.

I sighed and paced over to the window and peered out at the other buildings. "I figured my mother would be the only hurdle to jump, but now this."

"Miriam scares me." Brooks agreed, and Archer nodded. "I do not know how you're going to get her to agree to let you remodel your dad's building."

"I'm sure *she* won't be too much of a problem, but this…" I stalked back, eyeing the model and determined nothing would deter my plans. "No, there has to be a way, and I'll find it. I'll talk to Doug. You just take that black box off."

I peeked at the time on my watch as a notification arrived for a meeting with the engineering department back at Buchanan's, another meeting I didn't want to attend. I really needed to talk to my assistant, Pearl, about scheduling.

"We can't wait to hear how you pull this whole thing off. If anyone can, it's you, Rex." Archer set the pointer down.

"I have to go, but this is great work, guys. Beautiful." Again, I sort of gushed as I took one last look at the model, then left. Brooks followed me out to the elevators.

"Hey, I told your assistant to put me on your social calendar next week," he said.

"Oh yeah? Want to hit the new wine bar Jameson opened on 5th?" Our buddy spent a year touring the best wineries in the world and I'd been looking forward to supporting him.

"Maybe, but first, I told Archer you and I would be his wingmen at one of those speed dating events."

I practically punched the down arrow button on the wall. "Why the hell would you tell him that?"

"Come on, man, you know he's been in a slump since

Brianne left him last year. He's finally admitting he's ready to move on and wants to give this a try."

"Surely there must be a dozen other ways for a man of his caliber to meet the next love of his life."

"Oh yeah? Are you an expert on this topic?" He joked. He and my friends knew me too well. I had no plans to get tied down.

"You and Archer have fun, and meet me at the bar after." I left him hanging there and got on the elevator, escaping his smirk.

I had nothing against the institution of marriage, but with a mother like mine constantly pressuring me to settle down and pass on the Buchanan genes, I rebelled against anything that wasn't a quick one-night stand.

Ever since Richard's engagement fell apart, she'd been even worse—Attempting to sign me up for a millionaire matchmaking service, and calling me over for dinner where a friend's daughter just "happened" to be there.

No, now that I was on to her tricks to get me to tie the knot, I wouldn't give her the satisfaction. Marriage for me wouldn't happen anytime soon, no matter who fell into my path.

# 2

# 122 DAYS TO GO

## CHELSEA CALHOUN

*M*om squeezed me tight until I didn't think I could breathe anymore. She smelled heavenly, like the warm slices of cherry pie with vanilla ice cream she just served my sister, brother, and me in her diner, and the scent was all the things I loved about home in late August. I never wanted to forget this.

"I'm just moving to New York City. It's only a few hours' drive from here," I parted and reminded her.

Here being Holly Creek, the small town that's been my home for twenty-seven years, and today being officially the day I was finally off on a grand adventure. It was one I had put off since high school, but suddenly it was difficult to leave. We had been saying goodbye for an hour and were already behind schedule. At this pace, we'd be in the thick of city traffic when we arrived. Then again, when didn't the city have traffic?

Colt joined in the hug. My brother was so tall now he towered over us by at least a foot. He had grown into his handsome looks, with dark wavy hair and eyes of blue, just like our father—Dr. Oliver Calhoun, may he rest in peace.

"Oh, my Chelsea-Sunshine girl." Mom cried again, adjusting the sunflower in my hair.

Maisy, my impatient sister, honked the horn from my car parked in front of Flora's Diner, the restaurant my mother owned and had operated for as long as I can remember.

"Let's go, Chelsea. Love you, Mom. See you soon, Colt." She waved, letting her long, golden ponytail hang out the window.

"Yep. As soon as I can get this slave driver to let me have a weekend off," he elbowed Mom. "I'll come down to the city and raise hell with you all."

"Oh, how did this happen?" Mom cried into her apron—again. "You three once were my babies and now you're all adults. Soon you'll be bringing your babies to me—"

"Mom. Stop. None of us are having babies yet. Sheesh." Colt rolled his eyes. At twenty-one, he was still immature and having fun with girls his age in town, and needed several years to grow up before I could see him *ever* settling down and having children.

"You're already giving Mom a bad time? Maybe I shouldn't go," I teased, sort of.

"Chelsea Ruth Calhoun, you're going. And I won't hear another word about it." Mom wiped away the tears from her blue-green eyes and I thought that might be the end of them, since she used all three of my names. She was putting on a brave face now, and I must, too. "Go on, the city awaits. Oh, and here's a fresh box of chocolate chip cookies for you and Maisy-girl to share on the way."

Mom looked behind her at the deep windowsill of the diner, but there was no box sitting there.

"You mean these cookies?" Colt talked through a mouth full while holding out the box stamped with the Flora's Diner logo on top. I recalled making the new logo for Mom six years ago in one of the night classes I took at a nearby community college.

Between those classes and my years of working with her in the diner, I hoped I was prepared for what's coming next.

"Colt Jacob Calhoun, you give that box to your sister right now. As if you didn't sneak cookies all day as you worked, my goodness." Mom was all riled up now, and I chuckled at the camaraderie they shared. I wouldn't have left her high and dry like this, with just my brother to count on to help run the diner, but things have happened so fast the past two weeks.

Mom always says things happen in threes. In this case, three calls are what it took to start me off on a new adventure this fall.

It all started when Maisy, the smarty pants, made a frantic call home before the start of her fourth year at Columbia University, only two semesters away from graduating with her degree in neuroscience. She was going to share an apartment this year with her best friend, Sophie, a business major. To make ends meet, they searched for another roommate, and found one who was majoring in theater, but on moving day the actress-to-be cancelled.

I assured Maisy it wouldn't be the end of the world and to keep trying. Then the next day, a call came which none of us expected. Uncle Doug, our dad's brother, was in the hospital in NYC being treated for a heart condition, Aunt Louisa informed us. Mom fretted for her brother-in-law even though the doctors said he'd be okay, but would have to make some lifestyle changes. Louisa fretted about Sun-Up Deli, the Manhattan deli my uncle owned.

The third thing that happened was a dream come true. A week later, Uncle Doug called, resting at home after leaving the hospital. He asked if I'd help run his deli until his lease ran out New Year's Eve so he could take some time off to recuperate and plan for his retirement. Of course, Mom cried, but told me I had to do it because of the dream I put off so long ago for her.

That's how I found myself saying goodbye now to Mom,

Colt, and Holly Creek, heading to the big city. I'd miss this place, but I might be back come January. Meanwhile, I would have four months to live the life I always wanted and see where it would lead.

I even had a New York City bucket list of things I'd love to experience. Both fear and excitement rolled through me in a shiver. A lot could happen in one hundred and twenty-two days. I just needed to get in the car and drive away.

I took one last look at Mom with her shoulder length, red-dyed hair. She used to have a stunning red color naturally, like me, but the years added some gray. Now, she liked to say that her hair was enhanced. She looked fabulous since starting a new exercise regime two years ago at my urging, and hardly a trace existed anymore of the tired, depressed woman she'd become after Dad passed away.

I knew she and Colt would manage without me. I hoped.

"I'll text every day. Love you." I hurried to take the box of cookies before I cried again, or chickened out and changed my mind.

"Good luck, sweetie. I know you'll make great things happen. Be careful driving. Don't stop at the rest stops—"

"We'll be fine, Mom. Call you when we get there," Maisy, always little Miss Independent, yelled from the passenger seat.

"Scout out the bars and find the one with all the hot chicks for me, so we don't waste time when I come visit," Colt called after me. Mom elbowed him in the ribs. "Ow."

I got into the driver's side and honked as I pulled away. Maisy hung out the window and waved until Mom and Colt faded away in my rearview mirror.

"This will be so great," I said to Maisy as we passed the village green and the last shop on Main Street. But I didn't sound convinced, so I patted my pocket where I'd tucked a bucket list I'd scribbled with all the things I'd like to do while in the city. Maybe it was a silly thing to do, but it reminded me that whether this adventure was short term or long lasting, this was a chance for new experiences.

Tomorrow, I'd wake up and be more confident about the move, but not today, not when I had just left my heart behind and hadn't realized how hard that would be.

# 3

# BRIGHTEST SPOT

## REX

For the entire car ride into work this morning, I scrolled through all the important emails and messages my assistant Pearl had sent my way. There should be a rule against how many issues a CEO should have to deal with before noon. I paused scrolling at one thing that caught my eye and scowled, dialing her immediately.

"Good morning, Rex. How are you today?" Her usual sarcastic tone ripped through the phone. We had a love/hate relationship. She loved to torment me, and I hated her for it. But I couldn't do without her, being the former assistant to Richard. While he made himself scarce these days, Pearl was indispensable, as the resource I referred to most to navigate being a CEO of this damn family company.

"I'd like to know how speed dating got on my social calendar for tonight."

"Your friend called—the cute one, Brooks. He said he had something come up, and you had agreed to be Archer's wingman."

"No, I didn't. Take it off."

"You work too much, and you need to have some fun."

"You're giving me social advice now?"

"Seems to me you could use it."

"Remove it now," I ordered.

"And let poor Archer down? Nope. Call your friend and cancel it yourself." She hung up on me. Dammit, she's getting a little too comfortable in her role, knowing I couldn't do this job without her. Pearl was Dad's assistant before Richard's, practically family, and I couldn't fire her or my mother would kill me.

"We're here sir," Stephen said, pulling the car up to the curb in *front* of the Buchanan building instead of the back like usual. Too many people entered the front, and combined with the dingy decor and all the memories it scrounged up, if I had to walk through the lobby, it started my day off wrong. Today, for some reason, people were everywhere, waiting in line for something.

"You know I prefer to be dropped off in the back," I reminded him.

"Sorry, sir, but they're paving the road today, so I have to drop you here," he said.

"Fine, but why are all these people hanging about?"

"Oh, it's the deli. I hear they have a new menu now. People have been raving about it."

"What? Er, fine, Stephen. Thanks." I climbed out of the car and immediately my eyes wandered to the corner of my building and the biggest eyesore on the block. Only now the exterior of the deli appeared different, with red and white striped awnings and large pots of flowers in fall colors and a huge sandwich board announcing the daily special. People lined up to get inside and the tables were full.

"What the hell?" Well, this wouldn't do at all. It's time I had a talk with Doug Calhoun, man to man, and get him to agree to move on somewhere else. As I drew closer and saw people packed into the little deli, this *must* violate a fire code. Now *this* could play to my advantage. If I make old Doug's life miserable at the deli, he'd move on and exit this ridiculous lease agreement my father should never have signed.

I stood out front and called my friend in the fire department to report this. "Aiden? Rex here. I need a favor."

"I don't know, mate. The last favor I did for you almost cost me my job." The Australian-Irish man's interesting combined accent shot loudly through my phone.

"I'll throw in a bottle of rare Irish whiskey. Now, I think the deli in the Buchanan building is violating some codes. How quick can you get here?"

"Your building? Okay, I happen to be down a block, finishing up an inspection. I'll be right over."

"Thanks." It paid to know people in this city, as my father always said.

I waited several minutes, but the line only got longer. What the hell? Did people not eat breakfast and make coffee at home these days? Well, they'd have to soon enough because there's no way I'd let this deli stop my plans for the remodel of the building.

Screw this. I took a deep breath, and I stomped inside and pushed past everyone to the front of the line. I noticed a perky redhead behind the counter and snickered. Maybe *she* was the one attracting more people.

"Where's Doug Calhoun? I need to speak with him." With a gruff manner, I interrupted a stout man placing an order with the redhead at the register. No one ever awarded me for my people skills.

"And I need to speak to the Pope. Get outta here." The customer spoke with a thick New York Italian accent and thumbed toward the back.

"Sir, Doug's not here, but if you'd like to order breakfast or coffee, please take your place at the back of the line like everyone else. Thank you." The woman spoke with a melodic-like voice, and with red lipstick and bright green eyes, her smile beamed. Was she trying to kill me with kindness? New Yorkers didn't smile.

I'd never seen her before, not that I entered this deli often. Or ever. Some people had weird phobias about things, mine was about delis. I couldn't stand them, and for good reason.

"When will he be back?" I interrupted again.

She fluttered her lashes at me. Her name tag read Chelsea, and her hair flounced as she motioned to the one seat available in the entire place. "If you'll have a seat over there, I'll be right with you in a few minutes."

I huffed away; what choice did I have? I sat impatiently and looked at my watch. Aiden pinged he'd be here in about ten minutes. That wouldn't be soon enough.

I looked around the small space, cramped with people at tables and chairs, and the walls stuffed floor to ceiling with shelves and various food and sundries for sale. A bead of sweat formed on my brow and I loosened my tie.

The workers were visible at prep counters assembling sandwiches. Normally my favorite, I eyed the pastrami stacked high and my heart raced. Breathing in through my nose and out of my mouth only slowed old memories from crowding in. I needed something to ground me quickly, or I'd have a panic attack.

Then I zeroed in on *her*—Chelsea.

Her beauty radiated, almost too much for this old place, and what was with the red flower she wore tucking back the right side of her hair behind her ear? She twinkled and glowed at every customer with a friendliness that told me she was *no* New Yorker. If she were, she'd easily be the brightest spot in all the city.

I didn't know how many minutes passed by as I regulated my breathing and watched her effortless movements behind the counter, pouring coffee, chatting with customers, helping the other workers. Soon I realized the anxiety had lessened. Calmness overcame me until suddenly she walked up, took the vacated seat next to me, and placed a plate between us.

"Here. I brought you a blueberry muffin, fresh from the oven, and the best you'll ever have." As fruity and sweet as it smelled, I wouldn't dare touch it.

"I can't eat that," I grumbled.

"Oh. Okay." She appeared only momentarily deterred by my grumpy self, returning to that bright ray of sunshine with a smile that totally put me in the awkward place of wanting to both kiss her and push her away. "Now, about Uncle Doug—"

"He's your...Uncle?"

"Yes, the poor thing had some heart trouble. He needed some time away to get better, so I moved here to help."

"Moved from *where?*" I scowled.

"Holly Creek. The cutest small town in upstate New York you'll ever see." If it was possible, her eyes dazzled even more at the mention of her hometown. Damn, I'd hate to see her a year from now, when prolonged exposure to the city might have a way of turning her sour, snuffing out her light. "Have you been?"

"To Holly—er, no. Haven't had the pleasure." Then I recalled my purpose for being here. It certainly wasn't to get intrigued by this woman. I cleared my throat and shifted in my seat. "Doug's put in a long run here. He should retire and close this place down."

"He's thinking about it, but I'm hoping I can take it over. I've always dreamed of having a place like this all my own one day—"

"A deli?" I smirked.

"Sure, why not? I've worked at my mother's diner all my life. It was my dream to study at a culinary institute and eventually open my own restaurant, but...life has a way of not working out sometimes."

"Chelsea? This man is here to see you," one worker called to her, pointing at Aiden standing tall in his fireman's uniform.

"Oh, excuse me." She rushed over and left me, while Aiden winked my way. And now I felt like a heartless bastard. One who crushed a beautiful woman's day as I watched Aiden deliver the news, warning her with a citation that she couldn't have this many people occupying the space.

Damn the timing, but this was business, nothing personal. I didn't know her, and the less I knew about her, the better. Otherwise, forcing her out of my building would get complicated. Who needed complications? I left quickly, without looking back.

# 4

# RAKED BY REX

## CHELSEA

*I* slammed the door to our apartment and tossed a bag of sandwiches for dinner on the counter. With my hands on my hips, I stewed about the day, and paced the five steps between our tiny kitchen and our even smaller living room back and forth. I'd storm into my own bedroom, but Sophie was studying and sitting on it—the couch.

It turned out, New York apartments weren't flashy and big in our price range. Maisy and Sophie each had a matchbox sized room, while I rolled over a privacy screen and made my bed on the couch each night. Not convenient, but I didn't complain, considering this to be my only shot of beginning to live out my dream.

"Chels? What's wrong?" Maisy called from her stool, perched at the breakfast counter and what had become her desk.

"Just something happened today with a fireman," I explained.

"Ooh, was he handsome?" Sophie's dark eyebrows shot up, and her hazel eyes begged for details. The business major never missed a beat when it came to guys.

"Well, yes, he was, in fact, and he had this interesting accent—"

"What kind? Like dark and mysterious or—"

"Sophie, that's beside the point. It's what he did that irritated me." I spilled the events of the morning, with the mysterious man showing up asking for Uncle Doug one minute, and the appearance of the fireman the next.

I left out how gorgeous Mr. Mysterious was, though. I'd hoped to talk to him more, but he disappeared before I had the chance. In a city of millions of people, I'd probably never lay eyes on him again. But what did it matter? I wasn't here to fool around; I had work to do.

"This is just great. Two weeks in and I'm already getting cited for violating the fire code." I tossed my hands into the air and plopped onto the couch. "But I won't let anything stop me."

"That's it, boss girl. Stay determined." Maisy rushed over and sat on the floor in front of me, considering we had no other seats.

"I can't help it if word spreads fast about our new menu, drawing more people in every single day."

"I caught your social media post today and how you went live talking about the specials. You should do that daily," Sophie encouraged. She'd been a huge help to me modernizing Uncle Doug's deli with a new logo, and social media accounts. I also created a new menu, and had the red awnings installed outside. Doug supported whatever I wanted to do, and paid for the improvements.

It really surprised me. The pace of the city certainly moved faster than home. When Mom updated the menu at Flora's Diner a few years ago, hardly anyone noticed, and went right on ordering "their usual." Guess that's one difference between small town dining and here.

"Thanks. But what am I supposed to do, turn people away? If only I had a bigger place and more seating."

Maisy set a hand on my knee. "One step at a time, Chels. Someday soon you'll have your own place, I know it." Her support of my dreams encouraged me, especially considering I'd supported hers of going off to study neuroscience at an ivy league school. She took after our father, and being the ultra-smart one of the family, why shouldn't she get this degree and do something useful with it?

Sophie elbowed me in the ribs. "You know what time it is? Time to forget about all of this. We have that invitation to the speed dating event tonight, remember?" One of her friends worked as a DJ around the city and invited us. It sounded fun at the time, but now, I sighed, sinking back into the couch and could easily fall asleep any minute.

"I don't know. It's been a long day. I have to get up early tomorrow."

"No, come on. Don't pull that old lady crap on us," Maisy laughed. They loved to remind me I was five years older than them. "Moving to the city wasn't only for this opportunity to help Uncle Doug, but for the chance to experience things you wouldn't normally experience in Holly Creek."

"And that includes the New York City nightlife. So let's get all cute and head out the door before we're late." Sophie jumped off the couch and did a little celebration dance for us.

I laughed, and she was right. While I didn't really care to meet men, at least if things didn't turn out for me here with the deli, this would be my chance to enjoy everything the city offered.

"Uh, ladies, I think we're out of place here," I said two hours later as we walked into the swanky hotel in Manhattan for speed dating. Among the three of us, Sophie had the best clothes for going out to party at night, so we raided her closet and decided to go with a trio of sequined short gowns. Now, here we stood inside the door to the event, all glammed up and glitzy, staring at a room of people in navy or black suits, women and men both.

"Sophie! Hey girls. Glad you could make it. You look fabulous. Come on." Suz, the DJ, greeted us with a warm smile, despite her fierce look of purple hair shaved on the sides and slicked up in a faux-hawk with a leather vest, red plaid mini skirt, and slouchy socks ending at the Moto boots. She led us over to her setup with a turntable and speakers and such, all connected to her laptop. Since I moved here, we'd already taken up her invitations to two other clubs and had a great time. It certainly paid to know a DJ.

The lights dimmed right then, but it didn't stop me from tugging at my hemline, wishing it to grow three inches longer. The green sequins set off my hair and eyes, but I couldn't imagine any man here taking me seriously in this getup. Oh well, it was only five minutes to endure with each person, then we could leave.

The emcee for the event explained how this would work, how the men would rotate from woman to woman and get five minutes with each. After the event, we could mingle and dance with people we found interesting.

The women randomly took seats on the outside of a double circle of chairs, while the men sat on the inside chairs. I found a seat and smiled at the professionalism of the women on each side of me, eyeing their conservative sheath dresses and pearl earrings.

The timer started, and for each of the five-minute sessions, I did my best to share a bit of myself and to learn about each of the men. I met a few that seemed nice who I might talk to later, but no one I'd write home to Mom about.

We came down to the final two rotations. Then *he* sat down in front of the woman to my left—my Mr. Mysterious from this morning—still dashing in his tailored suit, blue eyes, and wavy dark hair laying back just right. Every *good* thing I noticed about him at first glance in the deli.

"Hi," I gushed. He jerked, as if surprised to see me.

"Uh, hi." That was it from him. No smile. Nothing. I glanced quickly down at his name tag. It read:

*My Name Is: Bored.*

And under it in small letters he'd written:

*Actually, it's Rex, and you have five minutes to impress me.*

My eyes widened. Wow! Turned out I didn't need five minutes to judge Mr. Mysterious. In one second, he seemed like a pompous ass. Glad I found out now. Definitely not my type— not that I was looking for love or even for fun right now, and especially not with a hot man in a custom suit without a beating heart.

I turned my attention to the guy seated in front of me and I grinned at him. He smiled back, and I liked his square jawline with a little five o'clock shadow. He pushed his glasses up his nose and smoothed back his light brown hair. Then the five-minute timer started.

He cleared his throat and held out his hand. "Hi. I'm Archer."

First impression: he seemed sweet and maybe shy. I shook it politely. "I'm Chelsea. What do you do for a living?" We both asked that question at the same time and chuckled.

"You first," I said.

"I'm an architectural engineer."

"Fascinating. Um, I have no idea what that means."

"Well, it's—"

And that's where I sort of tuned him out and felt bad about it. Because to my left, Rex stated loud and clear for his date, "I'm Rex Buchanan, CEO of Buchanan Energy."

Buchanan...why did that name sound familiar? Then it clicked. Every morning when I arrived at work by six, I passed by the lit up sign for the energy company in front of the building. *He's* the CEO? Like head honcho, in charge of it all, and the big man on the executive floor?

"Your turn. What do you do, Chelsea?" Archer asked.

"Oh, um, I…work in the food industry."

Rex snorted and glared at me. "You could at least be truthful with my friend, even though this date lasts all of five minutes."

"Excuse me, that's rude. *I'm* your date. Don't interrupt theirs," the woman in front of him huffed.

"What? I'm just being a good wingman to my buddy," Rex retorted.

I ignored him, then smiled again at Archer, trying to recover from Rex's interruption. "I used to manage my mother's diner and now I've taken over my uncle's deli for a little while. Do you have any siblings?"

"A couple of brothers. Brooks and I are twins and partners in our own architectural firm. Our youngest brother, Tucker, plays hockey and took off out west playing for a semi-pro team, and vows never to return back east. How about you?"

"Yes. Colt back home in Holly Creek. And Maisy is here with me tonight."

"Oh, Maisy." His face and eyes lit up. Interesting. "Yes, I was hoping to talk with her later. I'm a graduate of Columbia, so we have that in common. I gathered in my five minutes with her, she seems to love the city more than her hometown."

While it stabbed me in the heart to hear, it hardly surprised me. Maisy often talked about a bigger life far away from home. "Yes, in our family, she's the one most likely to travel the world." And in the remaining few minutes with him, I answered every question he had about her. I didn't mind though, and actually kind of enjoyed being able to assess him before I let him anywhere near my sister.

When the timer was up, the men rotated one last time, and I finally came face to face with Rex. I should run away, but *he* didn't. He sat down with his smoldering half smile as his eyes raked over me. Was I supposed to find his attention appealing?

My stomach flipped. It just so happened, deep down, I did.

# 5

## SPEED DATE

### REX

*I* was here for Archer, that's all. Speed dating wasn't my thing. I'd told him earlier I'd suffer through this night for his sake. Plus, I warned him he'd better make a connection with someone because my time as his wingman was valuable.

All that aside, I really felt for the guy. His ex did a number on him, stringing him along on an engagement that lasted a few years without setting a wedding date. She blamed it on the stress of graduate school, which he helped put her through. Next thing he knew, she was pregnant—but it wasn't his—and she moved in with her professor.

As much as I complained about having to take part in speed dating as his wingman, I would do anything to help him or any of my buddies. But I wouldn't have agreed to this had I known Chelsea would be here. I didn't need five minutes with her, not when I had a building to remodel and no plans for a deli in sight.

It was a damn shame, too, because sitting before her, I knew she was exactly my type. Any other time, another place, I'd take hours to explore her rare beauty and uncover every mystery within her shining emerald eyes. I'd find a million ways to recreate that blush of pink tainting her ivory complexion, appearing since I sat.

Like all my other dates, I'd have a night of passion, exploring her curvy body, giving her a time she'd never forget. Then I'd be on my merry way the morning after, completely satisfied, and I'd move on.

The bell rang for our speed date to begin and, for the first time ever with a woman, I had no strategy, no pickup line, nothing. With her pouty lips painted an electric red, matching the glossy sheen of her fingernails clicking away at the stem of her wineglass, they rendered me speechless.

Her hair fell like a curtain framing her face, red as if baptized in fire. The ends of the locks tickled the tops of her breasts, peeking out from her dress. And were probably silky to the touch—but I gripped the armrests of my seat so I wouldn't dare raise a hand to find out.

Thirty seconds were wasted ogling and assessing her, then finally she spoke, pointing to my name tag.

"Well, Rex, I must be impressing you because your eyes haven't left my cleavage yet."

I cleared my throat and straightened. "It's um...the sequins. They're glaring in the light."

"Sure. I suppose anything other than the drab corporate black and navy-blue would be blinding to someone who doesn't come down from the top of Buchanan tower much."

My lips quirked at her snarky attitude—although she delivered it with a sly smile—and I leaned to the right, casually draping my elbow over the back of my chair. "I grace people with my presence now and then."

"So I should feel honored you entered my deli this morning?"

"Especially. I don't like delis." I didn't mean for that to slip out the way it did. Very few people knew the trauma that particular deli caused me when I was little.

She snorted. "Because they're beneath you?"

"Well, the lobby *is* forty stories down from my corner office."

She chuckled and shook her head. "You are something else. I don't think I've ever met someone so full of himself, which is surprising since my Uncle Doug always talked about Mr. Buchanan like he was a sweet old man, and treated him like family."

Ouch. She couldn't have found a bigger knife to stab me with. "Sorry if I haven't given you a more favorable impression of me." And it was better this way, anyway. Finding ways to kick a certain beauty out of my building would be so much harder if I knew the tantalizing taste of her lips.

"Doesn't matter. I really didn't come to this speed dating event with any expectations. My sister and her friend wanted to try it, and right now, I'm all about experiencing the city when I'm not working," she replied.

"Oh, that's right. You left the small town behind to venture here. So, how are you finding New York City?"

A flash of red fingernails raked her locks behind one ear, showing off a small dangling gold hoop from an earlobe made for kissing. Shame I wouldn't be the man kissing it.

She shrugged. "Pricey. Crowded. Busy. But there's an energy here I don't find back home, like a constant hum underlying everything."

"This city never, ever sleeps, so they say."

"Now you're quoting a cheesy line from a famous song about the city?" Her tease amused me.

"I'd bet no one ever wrote a song about Honey Springs."

"Holly Creek," she corrected with a smirk. "If they did, it'd be a Christmas tune because the town takes its annual Christmas in July celebration very seriously. Oh, it's amazing, like right out of a Hallmark movie! Everything you'd want for the holidays. The scent of pumpkin pie, pine trees lit up everywhere, the songs of the season playing from speakers on the street, and a calendar packed with all sorts of festivities. The town is famous for our Christmas spirit," she finished with a dreamy look in her eyes.

Clearly, she loved Heart Falls, or wherever she was from. All the more reason she needed to go back to where she came from to be happy. Why, I'd be doing her a favor, forcing her out of the deli so she could do just that.

"Is the town famous or has it just found a way to capitalize on a holiday to bring in the tourists?" I countered skeptically.

She rolled her eyes while a corner of her mouth lifted. "You can't believe a town could simply be a joy to visit for the friendly spirit and cheer the townspeople deliver?"

"Sure they can...while also selling all sorts of Christmas paraphernalia and fattening their wallets. It's marketing 101, sweetheart." I finished off my drink.

"I suppose they taught you that in whatever Ivy League school you attended?"

"Damn right. Graduated Columbia with an MBA. How about you?" God, I *was* sounding rather arrogant.

She crossed her arms. "I graduated from the school of life. I learned everything I need to know from running my mother's diner for years."

"And that makes you think you'd be able to run a successful deli in Manhattan?" I raised an eyebrow. Without sounding too patronizing, I knew she'd have her work cut out for her...not that I cared.

"I'll bet, while you were cramming for tests in some stuffy university library, I was dealing with real-life situations and trying to figure out how to please the public while still being profitable."

I hated to admit; she impressed me. "You're pretty confident of your experience, aren't you?"

Her chin tilted up. "I am. Food has always been a part of my life. Mom made cooking a fun family time, then when she opened the diner, that became a family affair, but so much more. The diner has always been the heart and soul of our community. That's why I couldn't leave when—"

"One minute left," the DJ announced, and the music faded back in.

She looked down, almost appearing sad, and when she emerged with a slight smile, blinking rapidly, her green eyes glistened brighter, as if wet briefly by tears. I held her gaze and couldn't look away, suddenly wanting anything to take away this sad moment for her.

"Anyway, Rex, our time's almost up. I don't know if I impressed you, but..." She shook her head and finished her wine.

I halfway hated for this to end. "Out of every woman in the room, you did, if it makes you feel better."

Her chuckle lightened her mood and a coy smile replaced any trace of sadness I thought was there. "So...you're saying you'd like to talk more during the mingling to follow?"

*Oh, yes.* Shit, I shouldn't, and needed a quick excuse. "Sorry. I have to rush out to...another date." Yep, that's the excuse guaranteed to put her off for good. Now I wasn't only arrogant, but a jerk, too.

As the timer buzzed and the volume of the music increased, she smacked her lips. We rose from our seats, like everyone else. Waitstaff brought out trays of hors d'oeuvres and people moved toward the bar for more alcohol to bolster them up for the next phase after speed dating—mingling and dancing.

"Well then," she stood and straightened her dress, but grinned at me, still killing me with her small town kindness. "See you around, I guess."

I nodded and watched her sashay away, with a full view of her nice ass and lean legs, out of my life, and toward her friends.

Archer clapped a hand on my shoulder. "I know who *I* want to talk with. *Maisy.* And it looked like you and her sister were having an interesting chat. Let's go over there before anyone else gets to them."

I caught Chelsea's gaze across the way and wished more than anything I could follow. "Yeah. Sorry, buddy. Something's come up. I need to head out."

"What? The night's just getting interesting. A wingman doesn't leave in the middle of—"

"Hey, guys. Sorry I'm late. Had a meeting I couldn't get out of." Just then, Brooks appeared at my side. Thank God. "How'd it go?"

"You're just in time to escort Archer to that sparkling group of ladies over there where he thinks he has a shot." I pointed Chelsea's way. She was hard to miss, as if the dance floor lighting orbited around her beauty. "I hereby relinquish my wingman duties. Good luck."

They protested, but I walked briskly away from them. Once I made it to the door, I peeked back. Archer and Brooks had joined the circle of sequined ladies. Whatever was said made laughter go up all around.

My jaw clicked at how close Brooks stood to Chelsea and the way he eyed her cleavage, almost like a dog with his tongue hanging out. But I certainly didn't have a reason to be jealous.

My hand was on the door handle, about to launch out of the room, when Chelsea caught my stare. A protracted gaze with a sly smile I could read so much more into, but I wouldn't. Business was always first, before pleasure. Dad taught me well.

Kicking the deli out of my building was my game, and I'd win. Later, when she'd no doubt be heartbroken, she could cry on my shoulder. Then I'd take her as my reward before she moved back to Honey Brook...or wherever it was she came from.

She could keep her Christmas spirit, and I'd have my father's building modernized without that damn deli in sight. We'd both end up happy. Somehow I'd make this happen, and, for once, it might be my best Christmas ever.

6

## NO RUSH

### CHELSEA

*A*s if still reeling from the speed date with Rex, every day I looked for him, hoping he'd stop by for a sandwich. Silly, really, when as CEO he probably had better things to do than eat lunch at a deli. Besides, he had rushed out for a date, and certainly hadn't bothered to come see me here again. I needed to forget him, and move on.

"There's our Chelsea-Sunshine," a man's voice called out from the front of the deli. I paused rolling out the perfect pie crust and glanced up. Very few people used the nickname my mother started long ago.

"Uncle Doug? Aunt Louisa? Hi! Come to check up on me? How are you feeling?" I came around the counter and barraged him with questions as I hugged his body, noting his frame felt smaller in my arms.

He leaned heavily on a glossy wooden cane of redwood with a brass holder, and it pained me to see him like this—almost like Dad before he passed away. Although there was a rose hue to Doug's cheeks, more white hair, and less dark circles under his eyes as opposed to when I first saw him in the hospital. Here's hoping he was on the mend.

"I'm doing swell. Don't fret over me. And since I have you here running things, I don't worry so much." The gravel in his old voice was probably about as cheerful as he could make it.

"Don't let him fool you," said Aunt Louisa. "He asks about you night and day, worried about this old place, but his blood pressure has improved."

"Hm. You can take the man out of the deli, but not the deli out of the man." I chuckled and took his hand in my elbow, and led him over to a nearby table to sit. At almost three on a Friday afternoon, the employees were busy closing for the day, so hardly anyone was around. And what a day it'd been. "Can I get you anything? Coffee? A muffin?"

"No, thanks. Sit, sit. Louisa showed me the website and new menu online with pies and more. Outstanding. I never cared for baking, but I know you have your mother's knack for it." The pride showing on his face did my heart good. "New Yorkers must like it because sales are way up. You might just be better at this than I was."

"Oh gosh, thanks, Uncle Doug." My hand flew to my heart. "That means so much to me. It's been a whirlwind of a month, for sure, but...I love it here. I think—" I glanced quickly around the shop that I'd already poured my heart and soul into, and gushed. "I think I'm ready to talk about renewing the lease."

"Whoa, whoa, hang on. While nothing would make me happier, this is just the honeymoon phase." He chuckled, shared a knowing look with Louisa, and squeezed her hand. My brows stitched together.

"What do you mean?"

"When we first opened this place, it was a dream for Doug, too. He loved it. But soon, as with anything in life or love, the bloom wears off a little, sweetie," Louisa explained, and I knew the look in her gray eyes was only one of concern. Plus, she likely had been talking to my mother, who would worry about me until she had no more breath left in her.

All things considered, it was going better than I expected. Monday through Friday, I woke up at the crack of dawn, caught the subway from the apartment to the deli, worked all day, and by the time we closed at 3 in the afternoon, I was exhausted. Over the weekends, I caught up on my sleep, but practically leapt out of bed Monday mornings for a repeat, and perfectly happy for it.

Then there was the city itself, with something to see or do daily. I didn't know how she did it, but Sophie scored cheap to free tickets to things left and right. Why, later tonight, we'd be attending the opera for free thanks to some tickets she got from a professor. All in all, I loved every minute of this adventure so far.

"What we're saying is, don't rush. You just got here. Enjoy the city, and do your best. Trust me, you'll have some challenging days ahead that might make you question things," Doug advised, with a voice so much like Dad, it was uncanny, and I missed him.

I could always count on my father to be a guiding voice, until the saddest day of my life when he passed away. All prepared I'd been to move the summer after high school to attend a culinary institute in New York City, but after news of his diagnosis of stage four cancer, I couldn't leave town.

I couldn't see leaving Holly Creek and my family behind at a time like that. Mom was a mess and Maisy and Colt, being years younger than me, needed help through it all. Dad needed his family around him. So I remained and put off my dreams in order to be there for everyone.

Now, I had an incredible second chance fall into my lap, and so far, it'd been what I always dreamed of. But I'd take the time like they asked, even though I already knew my heart. I also made a note to be a better niece and check on Doug and Louisa more often.

"Well, we did have a little difficulty today, but not to worry, nothing I couldn't overcome," I admitted, but quickly covered it with a smile.

"Trust me, I've seen and done it all over twenty years. Tell me what happened," Doug leaned forward.

"Really, I don't want to bother you."

"Now look, Chelsea, you've got him all riled up. He won't be able to sleep tonight unless you spill the beans," Louisa lamented, glaring over the top of her gold-rimmed glasses.

"Fine. It was no big deal, but our food delivery from Delaney's didn't arrive, and they claimed I never sent the order in, even though I am certain I did. They said they couldn't do anything about it and I'd have to wait until next week to place an order."

"What? Delaney's has never been difficult before. Me and old Delaney go way back; must be his nephews being such pricks taking over the business. Want I should give them a call?" Doug got bent out of shape about it, and there was Louisa's arm, holding him back.

"No, I handled it. Thankfully, between Sophie and Maisy, they gathered a bunch of their college mates and hit as many grocery stores as they could to help make up for it. Now I'm all stocked up until the next scheduled delivery, and I'll make double sure the orders go in the next time," I finished strongly, again covering up the challenge with a grin that split my face.

I still didn't understand how that happened. I knew I hit the submit button, but they claimed they never received the order. No matter. Things worked out, and I wouldn't dwell on it.

"Well, honey, one thing for sure is that you'll have a lot of ups and a few downs along the way. But I think you've got a good head on your shoulders for this. Keep enjoying the process." He leaned in with lips puckered, and I offered my cheek for the kiss.

"So, about the lease—"

He stopped me with his hands up. "We have until New Year's

Eve. No rush. Just keep doing the amazing job you're doing and we'll check in with you next month."

He was right, but that didn't stop my shoulders from drooping. We had time to think about things. No sense rushing. Besides, he didn't ask me about Mom or Colt or Holly Creek. If he had, I wouldn't have been able to cover up the fact that I missed them all terribly.

After they left, I finished baking up two peach pies for the day, ready for the next day's lunch rush, and checked myself in the mirror. Ever since Sophie helped me get started with a new social media page for the deli, I attempted to go live at least once daily with the special of the day or other news.

A quick glance assured me I had no flour on my cheek like the first time. And I undid an extra button on my blouse because *sex sells,* Sophie told me.

"Hello friends of the city. It's me, Chelsea, at the Sun-Up Deli, back again with some yummy treats." I hovered the camera showing me plus the pies on the old marble countertop, one of my favorite things here. Admittedly, the deli could use a remodel, and someday I hoped I could afford it, but some things would remain, like this marble slab, perfect for baking.

I zoomed in on the peach pies and took a whiff. "Mm. Fresh peaches ripe from the market today, and now ready to serve in pies by the slice. Let's try one, shall we?"

I already had a small slice on a delicate white china plate with frilly edges. I zoomed in again. "Look at that beautiful, flaky crust, dusted with sugar. I'm not even going to ruin this slice with whipped cream or ice cream, although you can if you order a slice tomorrow. Nope, today, I'm going straight to the flavor of peach pie in my bite."

Using my fork, I cut into the slice and put it in my mouth, closing my eyes and moaning for full effect. "Oh God. So good. You really must try this. My mouth is having an orgasm. Stop on by for lunch tomorrow and yours can, too."

My cheeks must be burning, but I continued on. "Buy any sandwich and add on a slice of pie for three dollars. But hurry, only two pies, so only sixteen slices—well, fifteen now. Mm." I stuffed another bite into my mouth, moaned and logged off.

I cringed, but marketing was necessary, and hopefully that would entice more customers to stop by, although I was getting to know our regulars and enjoyed each one. Yes, some had snarky New York attitudes, but I didn't let that stop me from putting a little love into each menu item we made.

I put the pies in the case, ready for tomorrow. My workers had all left for the day, and it was time to head home. At the door, with one last look around the deli, I nodded, satisfied with another day done.

I locked up and crossed the concourse of the Buchanan building, heading for the subway. Each afternoon since the speed date, I had peered up to the top of the building, wondering if Rex was up there somewhere looking down at me. But not this time. I was too proud of myself and full of hope for my future with the deli.

# 7

# IGNITED AT THE OPERA

## CHELSEA

*T*he usher walked us to our seats, getting closer and closer to the stage.

"Sophie, who did you say you got these tickets from?" I asked.

"My computer arts professor has a brother in the orchestra. She offered the tickets to whoever had the best score on the exam this week," she whispered.

Since there were only two tickets, Maisy said she didn't want to go, and I was so grateful for this opportunity to see my first opera. Tonight we chose elegant little black dresses to wear, and might actually fit in.

With our hair swept up off our necks and dangling pearl earrings, we wouldn't look too out of place among the patrons who appeared to be pretty dressed up, with men in their tuxedos and women in gowns, diamonds, and satin gloves.

No matter. Tonight, I would cross another thing off my New York City bucket list.

When the usher finally stopped at the front row—The. Front. Row.—he motioned to the last two empty seats on the aisle. I ducked in first, then Sophie after me. Once I settled, my elbow brushed the man sitting next to me and a ping of electricity startled me. I nervously smiled at the man to apologize—and it was Rex, looking about as shocked as I was to see him.

"Well, well. If it isn't the woman from Heart Acres." The corner of his mouth turned up.

"Rex. Oh. Wow." Our eyes met for a second, and that was all the time we had before the lights dimmed.

Sophie squeezed my arm on the other side of me and whispered, "Isn't this exciting?"

If exciting meant that my breath was taken away, seated next to the man I couldn't stop thinking about since our speed date, then yes, it was. Our conversation from that night replayed often in my head, usually on the subway to and from work, when I finally had a minute to myself to sit and do nothing. I laughed sometimes recalling Rex's arrogant replies and wondered if deep down he differed from the bold guy he put on for show in public.

I'd heard from Brooks, who had texted and asked me out for a drink twice since then, but I'd put him off. Meanwhile, Archer and Maisy seemed to be carrying on a relationship strictly by texting back and forth regularly. But Rex hadn't visited me again in the deli, and I certainly wasn't going all the way up to the fortieth floor if he wasn't interested in me. And why the hell did he matter to me, anyway?

But here I was, during the symphony introduction, and I could hardly pay attention, only fully aware of Rex's body heat. He leaned over our shared arm rest whispering, "First time?"

I sunk back a little. "Does it show? I wasn't sure what to wear."

A low chuckle came from his chest. "You look exquisite." His minty breath played across my neck and vied for attention with his spicy cologne. In his tux, that probably cost more than I made all month, he was properly dapper.

"I heard you had some trouble at the deli today. Everything okay?" He asked.

I jerked my head to look him square in the face. "How did you know?"

He shrugged. "My assistant said she heard something."

"Oh, yes. It was fine. Nothing I couldn't handle."

I crossed my legs and brushed his knee—big mistake. A fire ignited in my stomach, the likes of which I hadn't felt around a man in a long time. I bit my lip and squeezed my thighs tighter together for relief of aching need, convinced the man wore pheromone spritz. I shouldn't be attracted to Mr. Corner Office on the Fortieth Floor. Oh, how I was.

When the opera singers began, they mesmerized me, only I wished I knew the story and regretted not grabbing a program when Sophie and I arrived very last minute.

I didn't have to worry, though. Rex leaned my direction and whispered like a narrator, sharing the story with me while the operatic singers performed.

"This is a story of love and loss. The woman is penniless but falls for a rich man. The man can't acknowledge her though in public, despite his feelings for her. Tragically, the woman becomes ill and only he could afford the medicine she needs, but he doesn't provide it. Only in the end, beside her deathbed, does he regret not helping the love of his life."

My body reacted to his whispers with goosebumps spreading up and down my flesh. How in the world would I survive an entire night of this next to him?

It turned out I didn't have to. As soon as the curtains fell at the interval, he said something to the couple on his left about having an emergency and needing to leave. I stood from my seat to let him pass by, and as he did, I peered up into his eyes. He paused and looked down at me, with his mouth opened and about to say something, but instead nodded and continued on.

That was twice now he dashed away from me, which had to mean he wasn't interested, and probably had a girlfriend. I therefore gave my body permission to stop reacting to the man every time I saw him.

"Come on, girl. Let's get something to drink." Sophie pulled at my arm, totally unaware of the physical wreck Rex had left me in.

Our time in the lobby over a glass of champagne consisted mainly of people watching and making comments about someone's beautiful gown or another woman's diamonds. "Look at some of these men in their tuxes. They not only look like money, but they smell of it. How I'd love to have an affair with one, even a married one."

"Sophie!" I chuckled. Over the past month, Maisy and I had fun with her as our roommate. Living in the apartment with them was like a nonstop slumber party and we'd spent far too many nights up late gabbing about men and dreams.

"Seriously, though, like that man who sat next to you. Yummy. I'd love a billionaire bad boy treating me like a Pretty Woman, wouldn't you? At least for a fling. Not sure I want to get tied down right now. What about you?"

"Me?" I raised a brow.

"Yes, you, old woman. We need to find you a real man, because you work way too hard."

"I'm not really interested in dating or settling down right now. Not with the deli and all."

"I'm not talking about forever, just a fling. I see you with someone older, classy, rich. Let me see who we could bump into…"

As her eyes wandered the lobby hopping from man to man for me, I could only think of one irritatingly rich handsome man I'd even be remotely interested in for a fling. Rex. But that was silly. He's clearly not interested in me, and I didn't have time or energy to date, being solely focused on the deli right now. Besides, he was a big city guy too stuck on himself to see me.

# 8

# THE TROUBLE WITH PEARL

## REX

"Sir, we're passing by the deli," Stephen remarked, as I arrived late to work in what had become our ritual for drop off. Just a simple cruise by the front of my building to keep an eye on Chelsea—er, the deli.

"Thank you." I paused my phone scrolling to peer at the corner with the window half down, only to find changes once again. The deli was decorated out front with fake garlands of fall leaves, and pumpkins galore, plus three tables and chairs with red umbrellas, each seating for four, and, of course, they were full of people. "What the hell? Is that allowed? Can she put tables out front?"

"I'm not sure, sir," he answered, even though I didn't really expect him to know.

Then I spotted Pearl seated at one. "Stop. I'll get out here." I hustled out of the car and marched up to her. "Pearl, what are you doing here?"

"Oh, hi, Rex. Just enjoying the special of the day, a lovely Pastrami sandwich. You should try it, they put a unique spin on it—"

I scowled and thumbed to the side. "May I have a word over here, please?"

"Oh. Sure thing." She'd been talking to a few of the C-suite executives who all waved to me with their hands full of sandwiches.

I waved back and stepped aside with her, then I motioned in front of me with an arm sweep. "Tell me what you see here?"

"Is this a trick question?" she asked. I squinted at her.

"Do I look like I'm playing tricks today? And tread carefully because I'm in a mood." Ever since the night at the opera, I'd been in one long mood. Sitting an inch away from Chelsea did that to me, suffering while enveloped in her perfume, our arms and knees brushing, the way her nipples pebbled as I whispered the story in her ear. I didn't want to rush off halfway through, but I couldn't control a certain body part of mine who desired to make her acquaintance.

"Yes, I noticed that about you lately. Are you getting enough sleep?" Pearl dared ask.

"Answer the question," I said through gritted teeth.

"Hm. Well, I see Fall decor. Tables and chairs—"

"Exactly. And I'm pretty sure the lease agreement stipulates adding any seating outside requires permission from the management. So tell the management team to send her a notice that she's in violation." I unbuttoned my suit jacket and planted my hands on my hips, and glad I'd recently taken the time to review the old deli agreement. Ridiculous how much favor Dad had granted Doug Calhoun.

"But *you* gave her permission." She smirked.

"What? No, I didn't. Tell me who's in charge of leases in the building."

"You are." I glared at her. She continued, "A money-saving measure Richard put in place a few years ago was to run building management through the CEO's office. When you took over and I gave you the list of things you were responsible for as

CEO, you agreed to me acting on your behalf because you didn't want to deal with it. So, *you* did. She emailed asking for permission, and I answered for you."

I cocked my head and crossed my arms. "Dammit Pearl, you're a real pain in my ass, you know that?" In my periphery, Chelsea appeared, taking my attention away from this excruciating conversation with my irritating assistant.

"Will that be all, because I'd really like to finish this fabulous pastrami? Rex?" Pearl tried to get through as I was focused on a ray of sunshine on an otherwise overcast fall day.

I couldn't miss seeing Chelsea in her yellow dress hugging every curve as she moved gracefully from table to table, chatting and smiling at the patrons. The white apron she wore tied tight around her slender waist and Goddamn, I wanted to tug on that string at the low of her back.

A man stopped her with a comment, and they laughed together. My jaw clicked because I wanted to be that man, to be the *only* man seeing her, talking with her, making her laughter ring out. She was...lovely, and if she were a server in a fancy restaurant, she'd be the type that I'd tip generously...and ask for her phone number for a date.

She noticed me, smiled and waved, and I waved back, and Pearl witnessed the whole exchange.

"Oh...I see you've met Chelsea. Interesting." She waved too. "Hey Chelsea, can you come here?"

"No, wait, what are you doing—" Too late, the mistress of the deli was on her way over, sashaying toward us with a sunny grin and, as usual, a flower holding back her hair, sitting right above her left ear. I could make out the daisy as she got closer. What was it with this woman and flowers in her hair? Not complaining, because I secretly enjoyed her fresh style. She was unlike any woman I knew in New York City, and as the playboy of the Buchanan's, I'd known several.

"Hi, Chelsea. Rex was just admiring your...new tables," Pearl said, skating on very thin ice with me. "Weren't you, Rex?"

"Ah, yes. They add a certain sidewalk appeal, I suppose. And more seating means more customers and more profits." I attempted to veer the conversation toward the professional and readied an excuse for a quick exit.

"Absolutely. I can't thank you enough for letting me put these out here. The customers love them and it really helps with my overcrowding problem. I even invited the fire inspector back in and treated him to a sandwich and a slice of pie to make sure he gave the approval," she said.

My jaw set hearing Aiden was so easily swayed by food.

"Besides, when Pearl told me the real reason you hate delis, I figured the table seating outside would help, and then maybe you'd come down for lunch once in a while," she finished.

"The...*real*...reason?" I slid a finger between my neck and collar.

"Yes, but don't worry. The fact you're claustrophobic will stay just between us," she lowered her voice and winked.

"Claus—?" I scowled at Pearl. Now she was in big trouble. The first phone call I'd make today would be to Mom to beg her to let me fire her.

"In fact, you should come down for lunch *today*. I have a pastrami sandwich on special." Chelsea's words went right to my stomach, and it growled.

"Ooh, Rex loves a good pastrami, don't ya?" Pearl's irritating grin showed way too many teeth, getting too much satisfaction out of this conversation.

"As good as the next New Yorker, I suppose." I smirked.

"Then you must be sure to try mine. I make it extra special. This is not your ordinary sandwich. Oh, I have to go. Duty calls. See you soon." Chelsea wiggled her fingers in the air and off she went to clear one of the tables.

"Claustrophobia?" I raised a brow at Pearl.

"What? It's creative, don't you think? I was pretty sure you wouldn't want her to know why you *really* hate this deli, especially when she asked if you ever venture out for lunch…" Very few people knew my reasons, and that was exactly the way I preferred it. "Among other questions she had about you."

"Questions about me? Like what?"

"Just girl talk. Sounds to me like you two should get more acquainted." She took her phone out of her pocket and pulled up what looked like my schedule, and poised her finger, ready to type. "Shall I put in for a lunch date with Chelsea over the special of the day?"

"Absolutely not."

"Okay then. You're free for drinks next Tuesday after work."

"Shut it, Pearl. I'm not dating Chelsea."

"Why not? She's a beautiful woman, plus she knows her way around a kitchen. You'd never go hungry."

Because I couldn't see dating her and crushing her spirit at the same time; that would never work. Besides, I didn't date. I fucked around when it suited my purposes. I had my playboy reputation to live up to. "Enough. Don't you have work to do upstairs?"

"Yep. Especially since your mother is on her way to meet with you shortly."

I groaned and slapped my face, dragging my hand down my cheek. "You're just now reminding me?" But she didn't hear while heading back to her table to finish eating her lunch.

"Shit." Now I had no choice but to enter the building through the front lobby. I stood there and peered at the front entrance, trying to imagine the glass dome there Archer had designed. It'd be magnificent when complete.

Of course, that all depended upon getting Miriam Buchanan-Astor on my side with this plan. Almost like selling my soul to the devil, I wondered what Mom would make me agree to do to make that happen. Date a daughter of a friend of hers? Hell, even marry?

# 9

## MOTHER'S WISHES

### REX

*Y*ep, I was right. Mom wasn't interested at all in my new ideas for the building. In my office, she waved off the model of the lobby without a care for the time Brooks and Archer had poured into making it.

After unveiling my plan to remodel the lobby of the building to include shops and eateries, the best Manhattan could offer, something I figured would appeal to her ego and elevate her status among her society friends even more, she wouldn't hear of it.

"This was Patrick's first building, and I met him while it was being built," she recalled with a faraway look on her face, which hardly showed a wrinkle since she could afford the best in plastic surgery. "I'll not have you deface it. Every time I'm here, I remember when we dated, and he…he…"

"He took you to the rooftop the day the building was complete for a candlelight dinner and proposed to you." I filled in for her. Her tears started, and I held out a tissue from a box on my credenza. "I know, Mom. I've heard the story a million times. But it's just a building that needs updating. Your memories will stay intact."

She dabbed at her nose, making her huge diamond ring dazzle in the office light. Then she donned a steely gaze. "We may have had you and Richard late in life, but we were a family and shared so many good times. How can you be disrespectful and even think of changing what your father built?"

My jaw set. She was making this too personal when it was just good business. I took off my jacket, laying it over the back of my chair and countered, "*I'm* in control of the business now. You know I don't really need your approval."

"Oh, but in your heart, you know you do, which is why you're showing me these plans today," she seethed, squinting her hooded gray eyes at me with her heavily penciled brows scrunched. I swallowed hard but continued my own threats.

"I'm sure the board will approve it when I put it to the vote later this month."

She chuckled almost maniacally. "You forget, my dear boy. I put the majority of the board of directors in place and can call in all my favors to block you from moving forward with this. Besides, even the directors have grown tired of the Buchanan brothers and their playboy ways. Many of them are calling for an ultimatum that you settle down and marry. A playboy image doesn't suit the reputation of our long, illustrious company."

There we were, at odds. Miriam had been a force all our lives, and, not knocking how wonderful a mother she was, she'd been the one who ruled over dad and us. And now she's also throwing the directors into this fight? This time, I wouldn't back down.

"Dad is the entire reason I want this. You're right, he built a great company, but this building is old and tired. I want Dad's legacy to last."

"Now you're making *me* feel old and tired." She huffed.

"Let's face it, then. Soon none of us will be around, and I'd love nothing more than to leave this building more beautiful and updated for the next generation of Buchanan's to be proud of." *Oh shit.* I managed to bring up a touchy subject, and the second I did, I could see Miriam's wheels turning.

"Hah! Next generation? That would require you and Richard getting married and having children. Oh…Actually, that gives me an idea. Tell you what. When you get married, I'll let you remodel the building."

"That could take years," I spouted off.

"Doesn't have to. If you'd just stop being such a playboy, open yourself up to the possibility of meeting someone special, and let them into your heart, Rex.'

Why did my mind go forty stories down to a woman in a yellow dress with a daisy in her hair? I shook that thought out of my head. But then again…Mom posed a scenario I could live with. Was I willing to do whatever it takes to get what I want? Always.

"So what you're saying is, once I get married, you'll let me remodel the building? Deal. I'll open myself up. Would that make you happy?"

"Eventually. Now come over here, let's eat. I'm starving, and you look like you could use a little something yourself." From her oversized couture purse, she pulled a brown paper bag and sat at my little meeting table by the window. I sauntered over and joined her there, noticing the logo on the bag was from the Sun-Up Deli.

"What's this?"

She removed her Chanel scarf from around her neck and stowed it in her bag. "Pearl called and said the deli downstairs was having a pastrami special today and you hadn't eaten yet. Now sit."

Of course she did. I rolled my eyes and pulled out my chair. "I'd also like to talk to you about Pearl. Can I fire her?"

"Absolutely not. She's practically family. Patrick hired her and trained her, and after he passed on, she was Richard's right hand. And from what I can tell, you need her to be *both* your hands." She snidely remarked, then unwrapped her sandwich.

She took her first bite and moaned, closing her eyes while chewing. I always found it funny how much my high society mother loved a good deli sandwich just like my father did, but none of her friends knew about it, as she often dined with them on five star meals at some of New York's finest restaurants.

"Maybe that's the issue. I'm not cut out to be CEO." My comment interrupted her enjoyment.

Her eyes flashed open. "There has only ever been a Buchanan at the helm of this company and that's the way it'll stay. Now eat."

I reluctantly unwrapped and picked up the sandwich, inspecting what Chelsea did to it that made it so *special*. The iconic New York City sandwich was typically basic in nature, with pastrami, rye bread, and and a schmear of spicy brown mustard. Hers was definitely different.

With the meat packed on hearty onion bread, and layered with swiss cheese, the thick fatty slices combined with spicy brown mustard had my mouth watering. I dug my teeth into it, immediately transported to food heaven with the flavors combining deliciously in my mouth. I closed my eyes and moaned as well.

"Oh this is so good." Mom spoke after another mouthful. "I met Doug's niece, Chelsea, at the deli who told me about his heart condition. What a delightful girl she is?"

Damn, if Chelsea could impress Mom *and* make a sandwich this good…what else could she do? Every bite, I thought of her, savoring the flavors and taking my time, thinking only of what a night in bed with her might be like as Mom droned on and on about one thing or another.

It was only when she brought up the weekend's regatta in the Hamptons that I re-entered the conversation. "Marlena Tomason will be there. You remember her brother from school? Well, I'd like you two to meet at the party. We had lunch the other day, and she's working in PR now. Oh, she's lovely. We got along famously. She dresses well, carries herself well, and we even wore the same Louboutins that day," Miriam laughed.

Jeez, the last thing I needed was to date or marry a woman exactly like my mother. No. If I'm going to marry to get what I want, then I'll marry who I want. "Listen, I only planned to drive out for the regatta and come right back. I wasn't making a weekend of it," I said.

She finished her sandwich and sighed. "Why must this meeting with you today be so exhausting? You *know* we always host the annual regatta party at our Hampton's house."

I started to protest, but stopped as I took the last bite of my sandwich. A weekend away might help—so I could try to stop thinking about Chelsea. It's like I'd become obsessed ever since she showed up. She's the one thing standing in the way of my plans, but she's also the only woman I wanted. And that was a hard pill to swallow for a bachelor like me.

Meeting Marlena could also be an easy target for marriage. After all, it doesn't mean forever. Say I do, remodel the building, get a divorce, resume my playboy lifestyle. "Fine. I'll be at the party," I grumbled.

Mom gathered her scarf and purse, readying for her exit, but gave me a prolonged look. "As you say, I'm getting older. My heart hurts knowing you and Richard will be all alone when I die, so—"

"Stop. You're healthy, you have the best medical care your money can buy, and you'll live to be one hundred and twenty," I attempted reassurances, even reaching to give her a hug, despite the thick guilt trip she laid on. She stopped me with her hands up.

"Please, for me. Take this seriously. I've lost all hope for Richard, but you..." She cupped my cheek and gazed upon me with affectionate eyes. "You would make a wonderful husband and father someday—*soon.*"

"So I get married, and you let me remodel?"

She only smiled and gave my cheek a pat, then reached for her bag. "The party starts at seven. Be a good boy and be on time, and dress to impress like you always do."

Just like that, without giving me an answer, Miriam Buchanan-Astor left the building she loved so much, while I stewed in my office for another hour before deciding to go for a walk. I passed Pearl's desk on the way out and smirked. "Thanks for the pastrami. And change all my weekend plans. I'm going to the Hamptons."

"You're welcome, and I already did," she gloated. I snorted. Mom probably already clued her in about the weekend plans.

"Of course you did," I sighed, riding the elevator down forty floors, trying to clear my head. When I exited through the front doors, the late afternoon sunshine hit me, and for whatever reason, like the deli was suddenly the strongest magnet in the city, I was drawn to it. A peek inside the windows showed Chelsea moving about, then she spotted me.

She rushed out to greet me with a smile that could light up any dark cave on sheer energy alone. "Hi. We're closed, but I can get you something if you like. I made a fresh peach pie and there's two slices left."

No wonder the fruity scent of peaches teased my nose and my stomach the second she stepped out the door. My mouth watered, almost leaking with drool. "No, thanks. My mother brought me your pastrami sandwich."

"Oh?" She brightened, if it was possible for her to shine more. "How'd you like my take on it?"

Given the way she waited with her breath held and her expectant green eyes, I should tell her how incredible it was— best damn sandwich I'd had in a while. Better than sex, although my imagination ran wild thinking a night with her would top it.

But I held back my enthusiasm and grumbled. "The onion bread was an interesting choice."

Her shoulders fell a little, but she maintained her smile. "Wow. Tough critic. I entered it into New York City's best deli sandwich competition sponsored by the tourism agency. Let's hope it gets a better response there."

"Yeah, good luck." I shoved my hands into my pockets and stalked off.

I had half a mind to call my business associate who was on the board of the tourism agency to say they should think twice about awarding the honor to Sun-Up Deli.

Jeez, I couldn't be that much of a bastard, could I? I'd already tried calling the fire inspector on her, and messed with her deliveries through my buddy at Delaney's, but this? No, I couldn't do that to her; she doesn't deserve it. And I sort of have a soft spot for pretty redheads.

Two blocks away and I was still kicking my ass and rewarding myself for being the city's biggest jerk. If they had a contest for Jerk of New York, I'd win, hands down.

# 10

# BILLIONAIRE'S ARMS

## CHELSEA

*B*illionaire's Beach in the Hampton's was the last place I ever thought I'd get a chance to visit when I left Holly Creek. And, only possible because of an invite from Suz, our friendly, favorite DJ, who called and said she was part of the entertainment for some big fall party.

She needed a replacement for her assistant who had come down with a flu bug last minute, so Sophie was more than happy to take her place, and arranged for Maisy and I to tag along, too. We'd get to attend the fancy party, and she might have mentioned something about a boat race, too.

I fussed about leaving, at first, drained from working so hard, although loving it. But also something else bugged me— the way Rex walked away from the deli last night—and I stewed about it ever since. When he hardly reacted to the extra flare I put into the sandwich, it hurt. I thought he'd at least be decent and encouraging when he heard the news about my entry into the sandwich contest. Why did *his* opinion matter so much?

Suddenly, the idea of leaving the city for a quick getaway appealed. I needed to get Rex as far away from my mind as possible, and nothing would soothe me more than to walk along the beach, with my feet in the sand and dip my toes in the water. That's something I couldn't get from Holly Creek, for sure.

We threw clothes into overnight bags and drove through Long Island to Southampton. Along the way, the drive impressed me not only because of the magnificent homes and views, but also the little orchards and wineries. Still, as beautiful as everything was, it couldn't compare with home.

Holly Creek would always hold my heart, with the four seasons and the natural beauty around us. This time of year, the fall leaves would start to change, about to give the greatest show with oranges, reds, and yellows. But more than that, home will always be the people, my family there.

I missed home and the little farmhouse we grew up in. How quiet it must be now with only Mom and Colt there. We texted almost every day, even if there was nothing new to report, and Maisy and I called each Sunday. Mom said they were getting along fine. Colt complained Mom was smothering him, but I knew he'd miss her if he was miles and miles away.

"We're finally here, according to GPS," I announced, and turned in through the gate of the address Suz provided. Up ahead, at the center of a circular drive, a magnificent Shaker shingle-sided home appeared. My mouth dropped, counting the white framed windows three stories high, plus a level below like a daylight basement. "Oh, my God. Is this where the party will be tonight?"

"Yes, but there's a guest house over to the right, Suz said, where our room is...Oh my God." Like me, she and Maisy dropped their jaws, because the guest house was about the same size as the main house, but only two stories tall, not three, and between them both likely thousands of square feet.

"It's safe to say we're far from home," Maisy whispered in awe.

Suz met us out front, rocking hot pink hair and a black

leather off the shoulder dress. I admired her ability to pull-off her fierce looks every time we saw her.

"Ladies! You're here. Give the keys to the valet and I'll show you to your room." Walking through the house was like entering a whole new world. Everything was picture perfect, decorated in white fabrics and furniture of dark wood and shining white walls with dark beams overhead. I was afraid to touch anything.

Our room was in the workers' wing. I expected something tiny, like our city apartment, but not plush accommodations like these. A fluffy king size bed took up part of the room, and two couches facing each other by the window overlooked the...I ran to it and looked out at the most gorgeous view of the ocean. No wonder people loved beachfront property.

"Will this be okay? It'll have to be all four of us sleeping in one room, but hey, this party could last into the early morning hours, so by the time we crash, we won't care where we sleep." Suz laughed.

"I'll sleep on the beach for all I care. I hear this is unseasonably warm for the beginning of October," I tore myself from the view and tackled my bag, worried once again I didn't bring the right thing to wear for the caliber of this party.

"Well, have fun. Be sure to explore the grounds and enjoy. Hey Sophie, ready? I only have a couple of hours to go and need to get set up." Suz thumbed toward the door. The second they left, Maisy flew to the bed, landing in the middle and sinking down like it was a fluffy cloud.

"Ah. Wake me in a few hours when it's time to party," she exclaimed, wrapping her fingers behind her head. Poor girl had been studying so hard lately, I didn't blame her for wanting to rest.

"I'm going to see if I can meander to the beach. I'll be back later." Maisy barely noticed me walking out the door.

With so much activity going on setting up for the party, I steered clear of the main house. Who lives here? Seriously, though, it seemed a little too much. I never gave much thought to being filthy rich. I simply needed enough to be comfortable.

I kept following the path toward the ocean, and eventually I arrived there. Once I flipped off my sandals, the sand beneath my toes grounded me, tying me to the earth, in a feeling so surreal—I couldn't believe this was my life right now. I even rolled up the legs of my jeans and dared poke toes in the cold water.

For a while, I sat, just watching the waves roll in, simply being one with time and motion. With all the hustle I'd put into the deli since arriving in the city, the peaceful moment to relax in a place like this did my soul good. How fortunate were the people here who get to enjoy it as their backyard?

The sunlight, sand, and surf did wonders. After a while, my mind engaged in thoughts about home and the people I loved, drifting eventually to Uncle Doug and the deli, even Rex popped in, taking up space with his handsome looks and grumbly voice.

Why him? He'd left so abruptly—again—from the deli yesterday, I should put him right out of my mind.

"Ugh," I sighed back into the sand, closed my eyes, and wished I could.

AT THE PARTY, I fit right in with my short satin wrap dress the color of butterscotch paired with tortoise shell strappy sandals. Both things I picked up from a little boutique near our apartment. Maisy looked casually chic in a strapless floral maxi dress. We waved to Sophie and Suz and then tried to find the bar.

No matter how we dressed, at a party like this, I still felt out of place. So many people crowded into the space on the sprawling green lawn, spilling over to the pool area, and eventually a bar was in sight.

"Is that Archer?" Maisy gasped, pointing to the side while we waited in the long line. "And his brother?"

Sure enough, he and Brooks were standing nearby and spotted us. "Small world," Brooks called out, smiling and waving us over. We stepped out of the line and joined them.

"Yes, it is," Maisy gushed. The look on her face as she smiled coyly at Archer was returned by him. Hm. Guess something serious brewed between them, after all. I'd have to have a talk with her later about it. She was still young and just about to graduate. I hated for anything or anyone to hold her back from getting everything she ever wanted with her budding career.

After we told them how we ended up here, Brooks teased. "So, you're party crashers? Not to worry, I know the owner. I'll just tell him you're with me."

"I appreciate that," I laughed with him, noticing the twinkle in his hazel eyes for me. I liked him...as a friend. His reddish brown hair and whiskers with slight freckles across the nose were so boy-next-door cute...but he wasn't dashing. His friendliness and attentiveness were sweet, but he didn't make my heart go pitter-patter.

"Let's get you ladies some drinks. What'll you have?" He asked.

"Sex on the Beach." Maisy called out. Archer raised his brow with a crooked smile.

"Well, we're on Long Island, so...iced tea, please?" I asked, and the two men went to the line.

Maisy grabbed my arm. "Oh my God, Archer is *so* gorgeous. I can't believe he's here. I really like him." Oh no, her dreamy eyes were a huge flag.

"Sweetie, just take your time. Don't rush into anything. You have—"

"—your whole life ahead of you. Yeah, okay, mother hen." She smirked.

"Seriously, though, you are such a smart woman," I

complimented her, brushing her blonde curls over her shoulder. "I hate to see you put off your dreams for a man at this early stage of your life. Believe me, I put off all my dreams after Dad…and I don't regret it, but you have the chance to do big things at this stage of your life."

"Yes, like finally losing my virginity to a sexy older man." She winked at me, then trained her eyes on Archer again as they finally made it to the front of the line.

"Maisy-girl! Are you really thinking—"

"Hell, yes, I'm thinking. Chels, I'm almost done with college and I've never been so attracted to a man before, what with the way we talk and talk and how he makes me laugh. We get along so well, and I know it's all been by text, but now he's here. It's a sign. He has to be the one. Maybe not forever, who knows, but tonight…I think Archer will take really good care of me." She wiggled her eyebrows paired with a coy smile.

I shook my head, knowing I couldn't prevent my sister from doing what she wanted, but I at least could make sure she had protection because I knew she wasn't on the pill. "Do you have a condom?"

"Yes, Sophie filled my purse with some. Now stop fussing over me and worry about having a good time yourself. Brooks is so funny and cute. Honestly, if I hadn't met Archer first, I might have gone for him."

The brothers approached us with our drinks in hand and we chatted for a while. Archer had similar coloring as Brooks, but slightly darker, and while Brooks was a fun-loving, easy-going sort, Archer was an intellectual with a quietly keen sense of humor who could knock your socks off with a punchline and a devilish grin delivered at the right time.

I kept my eye on my sister, until finally Archer asked Maisy to dance. Surprisingly, he had some moves, and they were enjoying themselves. I guess she's right, that I shouldn't worry so much about her.

Brooks sighed and leaned in. "We may be twins, but I'm not a great dancer. Otherwise, I'd ask you—"

"Oh, no, it's okay. I'm not sure I could dance with these heels, anyway. I'd topple over."

"I'd catch you." Brooks stared into my eyes with so much intention in them, but I just...I couldn't return the look. And it wasn't fair to him, with so many other beautiful women around he could chase after. I should make it clear I see him only as a friend.

Suddenly, over his shoulder, I spotted Rex, focused on me with his dark eyes despite the gorgeous model-type woman he was standing with, who was trying to get his attention. My heart jumped...exactly the kind of reaction I'd been fighting every time he was anywhere near me. Brooks kept talking, but I couldn't hear a word, as if Rex held me under his spell.

It took some commotion from the dance floor to tear me away, finding a woman had interrupted Maisy and Archer. Clearly, he knew her because his face reacted, especially when the woman threw her arms around him. Maisy gasped.

Brooks reacted. "Oh shit. That's Archer's ex Brianne. He spent the past year pining away for her."

When the woman let him go, there were some words exchanged we couldn't hear, then she hooked her arm with his, and walked away with him...and Archer didn't bother to look back.

Maisy's face shattered, and she took off through the crowd.

"Maisy? Stop," I ran after her, but a surge of people blocked my way as a performer took the stage and music blared from huge speakers I hadn't noticed earlier. I pushed my way through the best I could, with my drink crashing to the ground as I got bumped along the way.

Brooks was behind me, yelling, "I'll help you find her!"

Finally, I reached the edge of the sea of people, with a lawn stretched before me. In the moonlight, I could see Maisy running toward the beach, pretty fast given her low-sandals as opposed to my heels. I stopped to take them off and Brooks passed me by.

"Don't worry. Let me talk to her and explain about Archer and his ex." He took off running before I could protest, so I brought out my phone from my pocket and texted her.

*Chelsea: Please come back. Let's talk.*

This played right into all my reasons for worrying about her, but I trusted Brooks to find her and bring her back.

"Is everything okay?" A deep voice behind me shocked me, and I turned right into the chest of Rex. My hands landed on his pecs and he caught me up, circling my arms in his grip. Breath escaped me as I tilted my face up, his mere inches away from mine. This close to him, my body tingled head to toe.

"Rex," I whispered.

"Chelsea," he whispered back. And my heart…pounded out of my chest.

# 11

# SHE ISN'T YOU

## REX

*M*arlena Tomason ended up an absolute bore, and much too similar to Mom for my tastes. Sure, she was satisfying to look at; a blonde bombshell wrapped up in expensive designer clothing, but not enough to keep my attention. For my mother's sake, though, I stayed the course.

My only goal for the night was simple: put on a show with Marlena to appease my mother enough that she would approve of my building renovations. And it was working, if the glow of approval from Mom's face indicated—until my eyes happened to land on Chelsea.

How the hell did *she* get here?

Across the party, standing with Brooks, her satin dress the color of butterscotch and silken red locks begged a touch. Her laughter rang out, and the air carried it to my ears like a song sung by angels. I shouldn't want to know what he said that made her laugh, and for me to be the only one making her laugh again, but I did. Why was I having this reaction to her every single time I saw her?

My brain went insane, fighting between keeping her away versus marching right over there, and convincing her she belonged with me. I had my plan, which didn't involve getting more complicated with her.

"Hm. She's pretty." Marlena followed my stare. "Who is she?"

"No one of consequence." I finish off my drink, but couldn't help glancing back at Chelsea again. Brooks whispered something in her ear and my knuckles turned white on my glass.

"You know, Rex. Let's cut the crap. Both our families want us married off. And people in our position are used to marriages of convenience. I need to marry before I'm thirty to get my trust fund. I don't know what you need, but if we help each other now, then later we both get what—or who—we want, right?" Marlena side-eyed me.

She was making sense, but I lost my mind altogether when Brooks touched Chelsea's arm. My jaw clicked, watching them together. Then Chelsea's eyes locked with mine, and nothing else in the world mattered but *her*.

Whatever Marlena talked about...*ignored.*

Remodel my building...*what building?*

Mom begging me to settle down and marry...Yeah, with the *right* woman, I just might. *Chelsea?*

A commotion on the dance floor stole my eyes away. I squinted and growled at Archer for being the cause, and vowed to make him pay later. But with his ex coming into view, I realized he had his hands full.

When Chelsea ran after her sister, with Brooks close on her heels, I wasn't about to lose sight of the redhead who had captivated me. I breezed past Marlena, shoving my drink into her hands, leaving her stunned behind me, and rushed out.

"Is everything okay?" I asked when I finally reached Chelsea. I must have stunned her because she turned right into me, her hands landing on my pecs, causing fireworks to shoot off in my brain. I caught her up, steadying her, gripping her arms. Her face tilted up, and fuck, my lips were inches away from tasting her. My cock twitched in my pants, begging to know every little thing about this woman that made my heart run wild.

"Rex," she whispered.

"Chelsea," I whispered back. "What are you doing at my party?"

She blinked a few times, then stepped back, out of my hold. "*Your* party?"

"This is my family home. Don't get me wrong, I'm happy to see you, just unexpected. Did you come with Brooks?" I smirked, still irritated.

Technically, she's mine. I saw and talked to Chelsea first. Hell, we even had a speed date, an entire five minutes of her all to myself, before Brooks came along. Surely, he would understand and back off.

Or wait—did Chelsea have a thing for Brooks?

"No. We came as guests of the DJ. I had no idea you or Brooks would even be here."

Thank fuck. "Can we talk?"

"Maybe later. Maisy's run off, upset at Archer's ex showing up. If you don't mind, I need to find her and make sure she's okay. I think she headed down to the beach." Her forehead lined with worry and concern for her sister—and that took precedence over anything else. I wasn't such a jerk that I couldn't put my needs aside for one minute, at least.

"Come on, I know a shortcut." Whatever possessed me, I grabbed her hand and led her through the gardens and out a path I'd traversed since a boy every summer vacation visiting the property. She didn't pull away, as if acknowledging to herself the hum of electricity sparking between our grip.

Something had been there with her since the beginning, teasing me to notice her, messing with me. Fuck, making me question my entire existence. I knew my reputation for being a billionaire playboy, and so did everyone else, as I'd lived it to the hilt for some time. But something about her made me want to slow down, take a long ride, and enjoy the view. My willpower to fight it wore thin.

Once we hit the beach, by the light of the moon, we stopped and looked up and down the shoreline, but no other shadowy figures were around. She pulled her hand away and texted someone. Damn, I wanted it back, but I peeked at the screen, where first the name of her sister lit up, then the name of Brooks last.

"Oh, where could she be?" she sighed. "Her face was so shocked. I can only imagine she's hurting. If your friend hadn't been leading her on when all this time he's been pining away for his ex—"

"Hey, I've known Archer for a long time. He's a good man. As far as I know, he was ready to get back out there and find someone new. He had no way of knowing his ex would show up tonight."

"If he's such a good friend of yours, then please tell him to back off. Maisy is much too smart with a big future ahead of her. She doesn't need a man holding her back."

"Wow. Overprotective much?" I regretted the tease when she rolled her eyes.

"Only because I know the pain of having your dreams interrupted." She heaved a sigh and trudged away in the sand, carrying her heels in her hand.

"Where are you going?"

"For a walk on the beach. At least that's *one* thing I'll get out of this trip to the Hamptons," she yelled.

"Wait up. You shouldn't walk alone." I kept pace with her.

"*Now* you want to stay with me? You left abruptly from the speed date, from the opera, and, yesterday, from the deli. That woman you were talking with at the party—is she your girlfriend?"

"I don't have a girlfriend."

"Your date then? Go on, run back to her."

"No. Not this time, because…"

"Because what, Rex?"

"Because she isn't *you*." I captured her arm and brought her close to me. My hand cupped the back of her neck, pulling her in, and my lips landed on hers. Possessed by something happening between us, or the stars or the moon, whatever the hell it was, I acted without thinking, taking what I'd wanted all along.

Warm, soft, so welcoming, her lips swelled from my attention. I pressed her closer to me, feeling every contour on her body touching mine. Her hands landed on my chest, cupping my pecs. As an ocean wave crashed onto the shore, my heart thundered in my ears. I grazed on the taste of her, sucking and kissing…until she pulled slightly away.

"You kissed me," she whispered.

"I did."

"I liked it."

"You did?"

"Yes." Her eyes shone like diamonds in the dark night, framed by fiery locks of hair. Never had a woman captivated me before her.

"There's more where that came from," I assured. Our lips melted together, burned by the flames between us. I craved all of her. From the beginning, I should have known better, thinking I could keep away. Forbidden by me and my greed, I wouldn't allow myself the pleasure of complicating things with her.

Now? The complications were only beginning.

# 12

# CLOSE QUARTERS

## CHELSEA

*T*he beach, moonlight, and kisses...some things to cross off of my New York City bucket list under the extra category of *Things I'd like to do if I'm ever in the Hamptons.*

Never in a billion years did I think it'd be possible with Rex. His kisses deserved an extra category all their own.

Perfect, sensual...leaving me breathless.

While this moment was everything, my mind raced ahead. What came next? A romp in the sand? Or maybe he'd take me into that enormous home and sweep me to his room for a night of fun?

His lips seared into my skin, trailing kisses down my neck. A thrill worked down my spine, centering between my legs at the attention he lavished, and my nipples peaked, begging for him to palm them. I clung to him for this, no matter where he took me.

Okay, maybe one night with Rex was exactly what I needed to get him out of my system. We were both adults, both busy with our careers, and if we consented and wanted it, why not?

My phone chirped, jolting me away from every nerve ending

in my body going crazy in his arms. I reluctantly worked out of them to read the message.

"Oh, it's Brooks. He says he found Maisy and they're talking. He'll get her back to the party soon." Another chime told me it was my sister. "And a text from her saying she'll be okay."

"Good. Now you can relax."

"Yes, true." The tension in my shoulders released. At least, I could relax about my sister. Spending more time with a man who had me on edge from the beginning was another matter. Inhaling the salty air, I gazed upon him. In the moonlight, he was even more dashing, especially with his sly smile.

Oh, I could do so many things with him, but a few seconds away was all I needed to bring me back to my senses. We'd essentially just met, and I rarely rushed these things. Always so busy with working at Mom's diner and now the deli to put too much stock into relationships.

I'd dated here and there back home, even tried a serious sort of boyfriend for a while, but work and my family needs came first. How can a man compete with that? Perhaps it was the same with Rex, being a busy CEO.

Rex pulled me to him again, but I put up a hand to stop him. Still, something about him was different, like the air surrounding him crackled with electricity. It drew me to him from first sight.

"I'd really like to walk along the beach in the moonlight and dip my toes in the water. It's on my bucket list for my time here in New York," I said, and legitimately, it was.

"Bucket list, huh?" He glanced back at the house and I almost thought he'd abandon me again. "Okay, hang on. I'll join you." He took off his shoes that looked made of expensive leather and set them in the sand. I dropped my heels beside them, then he rolled up his pant legs a little. We walked down to the water's edge, leaving the music and the party noise behind us, and traded for the sound of waves crashing on the shore.

"Beautiful night. The stars are so bright out here," I noticed, glancing up to the heavens. I never wanted to forget this moment.

"There's Orion's belt, see?" He pointed to the sky, but I had not a clue.

"Where? I don't know what I'm looking for?"

He came in close behind me and leaned down so we were almost cheek to cheek and eye level, pointing again. "There, see the three stars in a row? They're actually each bigger than the sun, and brighter, too. Did you know there are eighty eight constellations?"

His breath feathered across my cheek, and his lips hovered only inches away pointing out more stars. I desired the sexy man and his lips everywhere. But I continued walking to prolong the inevitable.

"How do you know so much about stars?" A breeze kicked up around us and I hugged my arms to my body.

"Old dreams of mastering the sea. I wanted to sail around the world as a boy and always researched it in my spare time. Finally, some years back, I almost did. Had everything planned to take a year and sail around the world."

"Really? What stopped you?" I quickly glanced at his face, but it proved a hard read.

"Time...age. Here, are you cold?" He removed his jacket and stood in front of me, draping it around my shoulders brushing his hands up and down my arms. "Better?"

"Oh yes, thanks."

He kissed my forehead sweetly and leaned down, brushing his lips along mine. Either his kisses or the gritty sand under my toes turning my feet freezing added a shiver down my spine. Only now did I realize the beach wasn't the best idea on a fall night like this. No wonder people weren't out here in droves, walking the beach at night.

"Have you sailed at all since?" I asked between kisses.

"I take my boat out a few times a year. I'll be sailing it in the regatta race tomorrow. Are you staying to watch?"

"Wait. You have a boat?"

"Yeah. Want to see it?"

"Oddly, I put sail on a boat on my wish list, but I was thinking more like the ferry that takes you across the harbor to see the Statue of Liberty."

"That's not a *real* boat." He chuckled like a man with a big ego. "We can take my car to the dock, if you're curious."

"Sure. I promised myself coming here that I'd live a little. Why not?"

"Okay, but first, let's dip your toes in the water, right? Come on." His evil grin as he pulled on my arm to the water made me believe he'd toss me in it.

"Oh, I'm fine. My toes are already frozen from the sand." I backed off.

"Nope, that won't do. If you're going to fulfill this bucket list, you do it all the way. Let me help you." He held out a hand. "Trust me."

Did I trust him? Something inside dared me to. I took his hand, and he led me back to the edge where the water crept up the shore.

Suddenly, he picked me up by circling his arms around my waist. I laughed and gazed down at him. "What are you doing?"

The sound of his feet sloshing in the water hit my ears. "Making this easier for you. I don't want you to miss out on a thing, Chelsea. Point your toes."

Slowly, he lowered me down his muscular body until my toes were in the freezing water. "Eep," I yelped and laughed.

"There. Now you're baptized by the holy water of the Hamptons." He chortled and carried me back several feet to the shore.

As he set me down, a grin split my face, and I was breathless. "Thank you, Rex." I reached up, cupped his cheeks, and pulled him in for another kiss. Because when would I have the chance to ever do this again?

A few minutes later, I stood with him in the seven car garage of the main house. "Take your pick," he said.

"*All* of these cars are yours?" I stared, wide-eyed. Rex and his family's money were too much.

"Not all. My mother's is the Rolls Royce. My brother, Richard, has those three there. I have these few here."

I pointed to a gray Italian-looking car. "That one?"

"Nice choice. That's one of my favorites, too."

Within in minutes, we headed down the road to the dock and his boat. The scent of the expensive leather seats with the cool wind whipping my hair overwhelmed, but, no matter how cold I was, the evening had been such a rush. I couldn't hold back. I waved my arms in the air and howled. Rex laughed, and I loved it.

"You're gorgeous letting go, you know that?" He complimented me.

My cheeks probably glowed pink under the moon. Something about the sea breeze in my hair and the man beside me had my heart racing as I hung my hand out and danced it on the wind.

"We're here," he announced, the ride over too early before it'd hardly begun.

We parked as the only car in the Hampton's Yacht Club lot this time of night, and walked to the docks, where several boats of different sizes all bobbed a little in the water.

"This one's mine." Rex pointed to a boat named *Ship Happened*. Of course, he had his own dock with a bigger boat than the rest. "Wait here."

He jumped on board and disappeared into the yacht and I waited a few minutes, eyeing the length of it. I thought he'd be racing some little sailboat, not a shiny white ship that must be a hundred feet long. I shook my head.

He's full of riches affording whatever he desired, so different from me working hard for what I needed or wanted. We definitely came from two different worlds.

He lowered a plank of some sort and held out a hand for me.

"Does size matter when it comes to sailing?" I teased.

"Size always matters when it comes to having the best of everything," came his sly smile and smart remark back. "Come on. I'll give you the grand tour."

From the control room to the lounge, someone had decorated everything with rich ebony wood and a decor of white and navy blue. My jaw hit the floor in the kitchen with every available amenity a chef would need.

"I could cook a feast here. Do you cook?" I asked.

He shrugged. "I hire a chef when I sail for more than a few days." Of course he did.

Next came the five bedrooms below deck. With lower ceilings and smaller but luxuriously furnished rooms, I started feeling closed in. I wasn't sure I could handle a week of sailing in this, one night, maybe, but any longer and I might end up sleeping on the deck. Then it occurred to me. "Wait…you have claustrophobia, but these rooms don't bother you?" I asked, squinting his direction.

He turned to face me with a deer in the headlights look and sighed. "I'm sorry Pearl told you that. It wasn't true."

I stepped back. "I don't understand. Then why don't you like coming into the deli?"

He shoved his hands into his pockets and lowered his gaze to the floor. "Dad took me to eat there as a boy, while he and Doug played poker in the back room. They played regularly after hours with some of their buddies."

He sat on the edge of the bed and leaned his elbows on his knees, still looking down. "I was eating some cookies, and I choked. By the time any of them noticed, I was blue and not breathing. Next thing I knew, I woke up in the hospital."

My hand flew to my heart, and I sunk into the bed next to him. "My God, Rex, I'm so sorry. You must have been so scared."

"Yeah, one of the most harrowing experiences of my life. I'm sorry, but I just can't enter the deli without having an anxiety attack. I know it's stupid. I'm a grown man, and it makes me sound weak."

"No, no. Not stupid at all. You're human. Nothing to be ashamed of." I couldn't help but rub his back, gliding my fingertips gently down his wall of muscles.

He shifted to face me. "Chelsea, the first day I saw you, I dared to go inside, but the walls caved in on me. Seeing you— the bright ray of sunshine you were behind the counter— grounded me and helped me get through it. For a few minutes, at least."

"Until you dashed out."

"Yeah." He reached up and fingered the locks of my hair away from my face. "But I won't be doing that again."

"Promise?"

His hand did that thing, sliding behind my neck, pulling me into him. The move was so sexy, and I bit my bottom lip.

"I fucking want you." He hovered before kissing me.

"What's stopping you from taking what you want?" God, if he didn't take me, I'd jump his bones. He had me that turned on right now with his vulnerability. How often did a billionaire sit next to me and reveal a secret anxiety he'd harbored for years and wanted to bed me?

The corner of his lips twitched. "There's something you should know about me, Chelsea. Nothing stops me from taking what I want. Ever."

His lips crashed onto mine, proving his point. The debonair billionaire set his sights on me and intended to take me. I had a feeling this night could be more than I ever dreamed possible, fulfilling more than what I wrote on my bucket list.

# 13

# VIXEN

## REX

*A*ll control I had before left me now. Our kisses deepened, devouring tongues. She clawed at the buttons of my shirt. I pulled at the tie of her dress. It opened, and I yanked the sleeves down, letting the fabric cascade to the floor.

Christ, the scent of her...sweet like vanilla mixed with sunshine, and if someone could figure out how to bottle it up, her scent might save the world.

My hands smoothed over the skin of her shoulders to her back, and with one twist of the clasp, her satin bra fell to the floor. I skimmed her torso with the back of my knuckles until my thumbs dove under the slinky straps of her panties. Down her thighs, I tugged them, and backed away a few feet. "Let me look at you."

The moonlight through the portal window made her creamy skin luminescent before me. Her full breasts perked with pink nipples like buds, waiting to flower with a touch of my tongue. Intense emerald eyes bore into me while she finished removing the scrap of satin and tossed it on the pile.

When she stood bare before me, my pulse raced from the full

sight of her, turning me into an animal, ready to attack. "You're fucking beautiful, you know that?"

"I like hearing *you* say so."

"Stay there," I ordered. I undid the rest of my shirt and threw it on her dress. My belt buckle came next, and I tore it through the belt loops. It landed with a crack on the floor, causing her to gasp. Then I knelt before her, with every intention of worshipping her while I had her in my grasp.

"I always know what I want, Chelsea." My tanned hands caressed up her creamy thighs. "But I need to hear you say the words." Her breath caught as I teased her thighs open, caressing the inside of them with my fingertips causing her flesh to break out with goosebumps.

"You, Rex. I want you," she moaned, and forced my hand directly on top of her mound, pushing me to feel her. The corner of my mouth twerked at her confidence. Had I met my match?

I slipped a finger through her wet seam, teasing my way through her folds until finding her hard nub, wet and waiting for me. My thumb strummed her clit. In my pants, my cock reached full thickness and there wasn't a damn thing I'd do about it—yet.

A peek at my hand revealed it damp and glistening. Her writhing at my touch with whimpers and moans drove me further, thrusting fingers inside her tight walls. They clamped down on me, and she ground into my hand.

"That's it, sweetness. When was the last time a man made you feel this good?" My ego needed the answer. Dying to watch her come undone, my arm swung around her hips, holding her in place so I could intensify my movements in and out of her slick core.

"A couple of years," she answered on a breathless whisper. Her hands threaded through my hair and our eyes locked. "How about you—your last time with a woman?"

"More recent than that."

"I figured you were a real playboy." She smirked.

"I am, and proud of it." I winked.

"The kind with a black book who keeps a regular schedule of women in and out of your room?"

"My book is blue," I quipped.

She huffed and pushed me away, and I chuckled and teetered off balance. But I scrambled up and caught her before she could reach the pile of clothes.

My arms circled her from behind, and she hissed. "You're a real rake, aren't you, Rex? Taking what you please. I'll bet women fall for you and you leave them all behind in your dust."

"Is that what you want? To fall for me and be the woman who could change my filthy ways?" I partly worried it might be true. My hand snaked back down the front of her, with thumb and forefinger massaging her clit. My other hand palmed her nipples and kneaded her breasts. She squirmed, held captive in my arms, and whimpered.

"Tell me you don't like this and I'll walk away, Chelsea. Tell me." I wanted her to push me away so I could sulk and force myself to do without her and not feel guilty at whatever I did to get what I wanted when I figured out how to push her out of the deli.

It didn't matter she knew *one* reason why I couldn't stand to be in the deli. There was another, and I'd use any means to rid myself of that place once and for all. My plans hadn't changed just because I was about to fuck her.

"Oh God," she moaned, her body shaking in my possession.

"No. *Oh Rex* should be the name you scream, and fuck, you're going to look so hot when you do." I clamped down on the delicate skin of her shoulder and sucked with every intention of leaving my mark.

"Your ego is huge."

"I have something even bigger to show you yet." My cock twitched in my pants against her back.

Her walls clenched around my fingers, spasming, but she bit her lips, refusing to scream. I pursued faster, harder, and finally she let go all control. "Rex! Yes."

I picked her up and carried her to my bed, splaying her out as she gathered the sheets in her fists and fought through her orgasm. Laying between her shaking thighs, I had my first taste of her...like raw honey, wild from the hive. I craved more.

"I won't stop until I have you coming undone two more times. Only then will you be stretched, and ready for me, sweetness. I know you have it in you, and I'll push you to the limit until I get what I want."

My tongue charged through her folds, finding her clit, and twirled around it.

"Rex! Damn you...but ooh..."

The combination of my tongue and fingers intensified to a peak and her second time coming undone eclipsed the first. I watched her beauty, her face contorting through the pleasurable sensations I brought her. I'd pay to see that face over and over all night long.

Right when I was ready to continue my pursuit for her third, suddenly, she pushed against me, and I fell to my back. She attacked my pants and pulled them and my boxers off, setting my huge member free. She stared and licked her lips, almost reward enough seeing her eyes aglow.

"And I like taking what I want, too. You think just because you're some big billionaire, you call all the shots?" Her coy smile —Damn, I liked this side of her.

"Condoms are in my wallet. Show me what you got." My hands laced behind my head and I watched with eager anticipation as she ripped a package open and sheathed me.

I almost came undone when she straddled me and my cock

nestled between her folds. She rode it for pressure on her clit. Taking what she wanted, her hands caressing her full breasts.

She was a sight I could see over and over again and never tire—and that was a huge problem. I held her at her waist as she ground on me to completion, shaking on top of me. Without being inside of her, I'd come myself any minute.

"That was incredible to watch you, sweetness. Fuck."

"Yes, we are fucking." Her brows wiggled with her coy smile, and her confidence did me in. She lined my sheathed cock up with her center and planted herself on me one inch at a time, proving the tightest fit.

The vixen in her came out to play tonight as she rocked to a perfect rhythm, and I hoped it was me, that I had this effect on her. I hated to think she was this way with every man who came before me. Dammit, I hated to think there'd be a man after me. I squeezed that thought out of my head.

"Mm. Sweetness, slow down," I warned. "I'm coming fast. You're too fucking tight—" Too late. Stars entered the corners of my vision. My toes curled, and I pressed her onto me and held her there, grunting my release, filling the condom with my seed.

She collapsed on top of me as if her bones were like warm honey, soft and sweet. Her hair in waves tickled my shoulder, but I didn't mind. We held there a while, simply calming our breathing. Then I shifted, laying her on the bed.

"I'll get something to clean us up." I tossed the condom into the garbage and retrieved a wet cloth. In the bathroom mirror, I smiled, but it was painful and double edged. One, more than pleased with our time together, the other...pissed at myself for taking this night away from her.

She could be out finding the man of her dreams, hell, even if it was with Brooks, instead of being with a man like me who was too set in his bachelor ways.

Unless...I could talk her into marriage. A convenient

arrangement where she'd help me win what I want and make my mother happy, and I'd give her something in return. Maybe let her lease one of the new restaurant spaces in the remodeled building. Or I could even set her up nicely with a deli space in one of the half dozen other buildings my family owned?

Yes, my mind raced with this plan. This could work. Hell, Chelsea and I get along well enough, it seemed, I could even see this lasting longer, as long as the arrangement suited us both. And she'd probably be a helluva lot more fun to hang around with than Marlena.

As I returned to the bed and cleaned her, she gazed appreciatively. This plan wasn't something I could spring upon her. It needed time to develop. How would I play this if I were really falling in love with her?

"That was nice of you. Thank you," she smiled. "How soon can we do it again?"

I chuckled, and wouldn't mind more of her tonight. "Soon. Give me a few minutes." I laid next to her and did something I *never* did with a woman after sex. I cuddled. And I...liked it. I liked *her* next to me, our bodies molding into each other. We laid a while, a knot of limbs, listening to the water slap against the boat, as she trailed a fingertip across my abs.

"Earlier tonight, you mentioned you know what it feels like to not pursue your dreams. We have that in common." I resisted the urge to sleep and instead thought of things to talk about to impress her.

She sighed. "After my dad passed away from cancer, my mom needed me to help her get through it, and Maisy and Colt were having a hard time in school." Her answer stunned me; it wasn't what I expected, and hit too close to home.

How two people from two different backgrounds could experience a similar heartbreak of losing our fathers to cancer was beyond me.

"My father was the town doctor for years, and much older

than my mother. But he wasn't rich from it. As a small town doctor, he often bartered for payments from patients who didn't have insurance, and even from some with. After a round of cancer treatments, the bills grew out of control. He wasn't able to keep up with things, and Mom had a time of it taking care of Dad. So I changed all my plans, and stayed in Holly Creek to help manage them and everything."

"What *were* your plans?" I asked. She laced her fingers with mine, and I didn't mind. In the past, I'd have run far away from a woman who'd get too close. But the urge didn't strike me now.

"Culinary school here in the city. Once I finished that, I wanted to go to Paris and study more there. Eventually, own my own pastry shop somewhere or back home." I shrugged. "I guess, now that I have Uncle Doug's deli to look after, my dreams came true in a round about way."

Guilt wracked through me about the deli and I grew quiet. And suddenly, the only thing I wanted in the world was to give Chelsea *everything* she wanted. What the hell was happening to me?

# 14

# NO WALK 'O SHAME HERE

## REX

*T*he boat groaned against the dock like people had just boarded. Then voices hit me. I shot straight up in bed, eyeing the sunlight through the porthole window.

"Shit." My eyes scanned for my clothes, finding them in a tangled mess on the floor with Chelsea's.

Moving beside me, she stirred. With the face of an angel surrounded by a carefree set of fiery locks, she opened her green eyes on me. Sexy bedroom eyes pointed right to my heart.

"What time is it?" She asked, her voice groggy and her lips swollen. I took full advantage of our night together and was damn proud of the way she looked this morning. Well-fucked.

Before I could answer, the guys sounded close and Brooks called out my name. "Rex? You down here? Awake?"

Xander laughed and said, "He's probably naked and passed out after fucking some woman all night."

"Shit. Remember that one time—" Archer began.

I cut him off right there, calling out through the door. "Hey assholes, give me some privacy, please?" I didn't need them telling Chelsea of my playboy not-so-distant past. Although after last night, she suspected it, anyway.

"Morning. Sorry. The guys are here, which means the race will start soon." I leaned down and sorted our clothes, handing hers to her.

"Oh, Maisy is probably worried sick about me." She searched through her things and produced a phone, texting away.

I got dressed quick and peaked out the porthole at the cloudless morning. "I'll take you to the house and be back in time for the race."

"No, it's fine. Stay. I'll call Maisy to come get me."

"I won't just leave you stranded. I guess you can take my car back to the house."

She froze after covering up her body with her dress. "Me? Drive your expensive luxury car?"

"Sure. It's only a car, Chelsea. Drives just like any other, so don't let the price tag scare you. Unfortunately, I probably should stay to prep for the race."

She chewed her cheek, getting dressed. "Fine."

But it wasn't fine, I could tell, from the way she tied the sash tight at her waist from her dress.

The guys made more noise above us, and I shot her an apologetic glance. "Guess the walk of shame won't be easy."

She glared. "You make what we did last night sound so cheap."

"No, not what I meant at all. If I had my way, I'd tell those idiots to piss off, hell I'd even cancel the race so I could get you back to your sister or spend more time with you."

She shook her head. "Don't worry about me. I'm a big girl. I wanted you last night, and I have no shame in that. I own my decisions."

She started toward the door, but I pulled her back to my front, my arms circled around her. "And I'm glad you did." I possessively held a hand to her throat and suckled on her earlobe and whispered. "I want to see you again."

"You do?"

"Yes. I might even walk into the deli and ask you out soon."

"So, you're saying I cured you of your phobia?" She grinned.

"Maybe. No promises." I slid my hand under her chin pushed her head back to my chest so our lips met again one more time before we hit the sunlight.

The instant we popped out of the stairwell, all the guys' heads turned our way, most with a grin and all-knowing sneer.

Two of them didn't appear happy.

"Chelsea?" Brooks exclaimed, his face reddening and jaw clicking upon seeing me holding her hand.

"Hi, Brooks. Thanks for taking care of Maisy last night." To her credit, she waved and passed on by, unaffected by the stares and whistles from the crew. We were quiet until reaching my car, and I let her in the driver's side, helping her adjust the seats, and buckle in. I pulled up the GPS for my home address.

I crouched down next to her. "You sure you'll be able to drive this powerful beast?"

"Yes. If I could handle a beast like you last night, I think I'll survive this drive." She grinned.

"True," I winked. "Both hands on the wheel now. Don't be throwing your hands in the air and howling like last night." My warning was rewarded by her laughter.

"Good luck at the race." She waved and drove off.

Damn, I really liked her. And fuck, the complications added up, crashing in.

I waited until she left the parking lot and turned onto the road before heading back to the boat.

Brooks stood at the entrance with his arms crossed. "What the fuck are you doing?"

"What's your problem, Brooks?"

"I guess I know why Chelsea turned me down for drinks—twice."

"I didn't know you liked her."

"Just tell me you're not using her, Rex. Because she's a nice woman, her sister, too. I spent all night talking with Maisy and learning about Chelsea's dreams with the deli. Does your plan involve getting her to fall for you so she'll quit the business?"

"It's not like that."

"I know you too damn well. If you string her along and dump her later, I'll lose all respect for you, man."

"That's not my plan." Now my head was too fucked up to think straight.

"Yeah right. You're saying you genuinely care for her?"

"Maybe. So?" My shoulders hit my ears.

He shook his head. "I don't believe you." He stalked off.

"Where are you going? What about the race?" He didn't respond. Well, this was a first, fighting with Brooks over a woman.

It took a team to race this boat together to win. Brody, Gage, and Xander, all college mates from Columbia, along with Archer and Brooks, made up my strong team, and we were on a winning streak the past few years; now we'd be lucky to finish today.

"Archer, are you staying?" I called to him.

"Yep. Whatever is going on between you two doesn't involve me." He shook his head.

"What happened with your ex last night?" I asked.

"What happened with you and Chelsea last night?" He countered.

We eyed each other, stayed mum, and got to work on the boat.

TOWARD THE END of the race, my boat was neck and neck with the competitors. Then I spotted Chelsea, Maisy, and their friends on the shore, rooting for my team. I encouraged the crew, all of us working harder less one man.

"Faster, guys. There's a bottle of Macallan for each of you when we win," I shouted.

"Something tells me he wants to show off with a win for that pretty redhead who's waving on the dock," Brody hollered.

"Oh yeah? Where'd you meet her, Rex?" Gage asked while manning the comms and keeping an eye out for the other boats. I said nothing.

Xander snickered. "Must be someone special. Usually you're boasting about your latest conquest."

"All right, enough. Let's win this fucking race," I snapped back, eyeing the steering compass. These guys were all some of my best friends, and I'd do anything for them, but sometimes they knew me too well.

It was touch and go, but finally we pulled just enough ahead to pass the final bouy and take the win. The guys cheered and high-fived. After we docked, I searched for Chelsea on the shore. She waved, but before I could reach her, other people crowded us.

When I finally glimpsed her again, she and her group drove away, headed back toward New York. If I thought about her often before, now I couldn't *stop* thinking about her...of everything I'd do to her if she were in my bed again...and of a proposition I'd have for her very soon.

# 15

# LADY IN RED

## CHELSEA

*R*ex had yet to walk into the deli and ask me out. I started hopeful every day and developed a nasty habit of checking the door each time the bells chimed, announcing another customer entering the deli.

By Friday, I resigned myself to being just another notch on this playboy's bedpost. I wasn't mad, exactly, just...disappointed. I enjoyed our night together in the Hamptons as much as I thought he did. Great sex was hard to come by these days. I guess I had hoped for something more.

Oh well. I peeked at my NYC bucket list where I'd hastily scrawled *Have a grand affair* at the very bottom as an after thought back in Holly Creek when I wrote it. If a one-night stand could be considered an affair, I snorted and crossed that achievement off the list as done.

I was about to do a pre-lunch post on social media about our hearty autumn beef soup special, when his assistant, Pearl, came in early before the lunch rush, having easily become one of the deli's regulars. She motioned me to the side.

"In case you've been wondering, I haven't ordered two

pastrami sandwiches all week because I have a huge appetite. Rex asked me each day to bring him one back."

"Oh? Why didn't he just come down and order one himself?"

"I don't know, but all week he's been really nervous, sweating about something, talking with his lawyer a lot, and I've heard your name mentioned a few times. I wondered if you knew what it was about."

"Me?" I wrinkled my forehead. "What would make you think I would know?"

"Well, he asked me to come down here and get your cell phone number today," she said, cocking her head and eyeing me. "But I told him to come down and ask for it himself."

"Oh, poor guy. I know he gets anxious about the deli. Here, I can give it to you for him." How silly of me to think I'd cured him of his deli issues? My heart surged, thinking all week he'd wanted to ask me out, but his anxiety stopped him.

She put a hand over mine before I could jot the number down. "Listen, honey. If my instincts are correct, I think he's smitten with you. The other bimbos he dated all catered to his whims. But you're different. Make him sweat a little." She wrinkled her nose and reached on the counter for one of the sandwiches, leaving the other. "Why not deliver his personally to his office?"

Smitten? Interesting. I kept playing over our time together on his boat, and how Rex knew his way around pleasuring a woman's body. And that's one reason I tried to keep myself in check, not letting thoughts run rampant.

I viewed him like a wild horse I wanted to tame and saddle. A horse-whisperer I wasn't though, and hardly had the answers how to do that. But I could certainly deliver his sandwich and see where we stood after finishing a live video post about our lunch special.

"Mm. Nothing beats the flavor for fall than a simmering

hearty soup." I zoomed the camera in on my spoon, stirring up the beautiful veggies. "Look at all the fresh vegetables that go into my recipe. And beef? Trust me, when you dip your spoon in for the first bite, you won't have to ask where the beef is because we put extra in it to—beef—it up." I chuckled at my joke.

I never wrote this stuff out, only winging it. I knew my cooking, and I knew good comfort food. That's all I needed to convince someone to try it.

I glanced at the names of people who watched my live video and commented, only to double take at a name. Dino B who wrote, *Hi Sweetness.* There's only one man who called me that. Could it be Rex Buchanan? As in Tyrannosaurus Rex—Dino B? Was he watching my social media accounts? Now I was even more self-conscious knowing he might be.

Was Pearl right and he was pining away for me way up there in his office? There was only one way to find out.

"I'll be back," I told Annie behind the counter, tearing off my apron, and grabbed Rex's sandwich. "Making a special delivery."

The entire way up the elevator, I thought about what I'd say to Rex. I needed a cute line, something that said I was just casually delivering this. No big deal, it doesn't mean we're an item or anything.

When Pearl ushered me right into his office with a knowing look, I burst in with a smile. "I have a hot pastrami sandwich, looking for a mouth to feed," only to find he was meeting with four other men in suits. Pearl closed the door behind me and left me standing there, stranded.

Each three-piece suited man stared at me, looking like I was from another planet. And I was, considering I'd worn my dress that was colored like candy corn with wide stripes of black on the bottom, orange in the middle and white on top, with black suede boots to my knees and a bright orange flower in my hair.

"Oh, I-I didn't realize you were in a meeting. I'll just drop this off here." I awkwardly tiptoed over to his desk and dropped his sandwich into the middle of it. He stared at me as if dumbfounded to see me.

I swiftly turned and headed for the door, but before I reached it, he ordered. "Everyone out—except you, Chelsea." I froze in place and watched the men dutifully empty the room.

Behind me, the footsteps rushing up to me from his pricey leather shoes matched the pace of my heart. His hands landed at my waist, and his body so close to mine caused a thrill up and down my spine.

He leaned in and whispered in my ear. "Fuck, it's good to see you."

"You could have seen me every day if you'd come down from your tower."

"I know. I had some...arrangements to make, and I was planning to come see you after you closed today. Come here." He turned me in one smooth move, wrapping me in his arms and taking my lips. My heart thumped so rapidly, it wouldn't have been possible to count the beats.

My hands landed at the back of his neck, fingering his short hair there. His suit felt like expensive fabric, probably made from a billion silkworms, and his cologne—Mm. Manly, seductive, powerful, just like Rex. I parted my lips, letting his tongue in, letting him claim me because the undeniable chemistry between us couldn't be ignored.

He pursued me until I couldn't possibly have any breath left in me. And when his lips finally parted from mine, I was jelly in his arms. My mind yelled, *Just take me, use me, do what you want with me.*

"Stay here." He growled and walked to the door only to lock it and return, as if he read my thoughts. Then he came up behind me again, only this time, his hands landed on my thighs, grazing my skin under the fabric of my dress and lifting it up, exposing the black lace of my panties. He palmed my buttocks and fingered the lace.

My breath hitched. "What are you doing, Rex?" I whispered.

"Tell me to stop, if that's what you want."

I didn't. I should return to the deli and help with the lunch rush, but he rendered me senseless with his attention. He shifted me toward the wall, my back landing against the wallpaper of golden stripes.

"That's my good girl," his voice, thick and sultry, praised me. He raised my arms above my head and pinned them there, claiming my lips again. His thigh shifted between my legs and I couldn't help myself. I ground against the silk and muscle, seeking relief, while the thickness in his pants hardened against my stomach.

He kissed down my neck to my cleavage, and I finally found my voice again, but only in a whisper. "What are you doing to me?"

"Whatever you want. Name it."

"I-I should go. It's lunch rush and the deli—"

"I can make this quick." His hand dove into my panties, rubbing circles on my clit. "Someone is wet. Tell me you've been thinking of me."

My thoughts stuttered, and I debated about giving him the satisfaction of knowing the answer, but my eyes betrayed me.

"Yeah, you have." Damn, he was so arrogant sometimes, and why did I find that so sexy? "Fuck, thoughts of you have plagued me all week. I can't stay away from your sweetness."

"Yet you have. I was beginning to think I was just another notch on your bedpost."

"No. You're not at all like the others. I'd burn the damn bedpost down for you."

I both hated hearing that and loved it at the same time. What if...what if things progressed between us? For the first time, I allowed myself to think beyond Christmas, to peek at a future with Rex. I'd have my deli, date Rex, enjoy living in the city. By this time next year, could I have Rex eating wedding cake out of my hands?

"Oh, God." I shuddered, my legs shaking, and squirmed in his hold as he pumped fingers in and out of me.

"No, remember? *Oh Rex,* is all you need to say."

"Your ego, I swear," I chuckled, riding the edge, about to crash land on the other side. I reached for his belt. "I want you inside of me."

He shoved my hand aside. "Later. Right now, this is all about you."

"You say later like you expect to see me or something." I was almost there. Another minute of this, and I'd be boneless in his hands.

"I do. I planned to ask you out tonight to a wine bar a buddy of mine just opened. Come with me. *Say yes.*"

Ooh, I was there and couldn't hold back. He had me feeling so good. "Yes. Oh Rex, yes." I moaned and broke in his arms, holding onto him for dear life.

"That's it sweetness. Let it all go." He held me close as the orgasm rolled through me. Only when my breathing returned to normal did he carry me to his private bathroom, setting me down carefully, kissing my wrists before he let me go. Without a word, he left me there to clean up.

Wow. He left me dizzy. I held onto the ledge of the sink and stared at myself in the gold-gilded mirror. The only remnant of my old life in Holly Creek was the silly dress I wore, surrounded by marble tile and all the luxury of his bathroom.

I could hardly believe this was my life right now, getting fingered in the executive suite by a billionaire playboy. But the heart desired what it desired, even if it made little sense.

When I exited, he was waiting for me with a smoldering grin. "*Come* and personally deliver my sandwiches anytime."

"Funny. But I'm just as busy as you are, so this won't be a regular thing. You should come down to see me."

"But the deli isn't as *private* as my office," his cheeky smile continued as he kissed my forehead. "About tonight...I'll pick you up at eight. Give Pearl your address."

"Okay. See you then." Still dazed from what had just happened, I managed to recite my address to Pearl's all-knowing smile. Rex's door was closed, so I asked her, "So, what would one wear on a date with Rex to a wine bar?"

"Black, honey. Everyone in New York wears black."

Black again...I fingered my bright dress on the elevator ride down. Guess I needed a whole new wardrobe to fit in with city life.

"Trust me, this outfit is perfect," Sophie beamed. "Especially for a date with a rich man."

"I don't know. I thought I should wear black." I twisted in the mirror to see all sides of me in the strapless red dress that hugged my curves. "Let me just wear that little dress I wore to the opera."

"Are you kidding? He's already seen you in that. No, red is the way to go. And you're not changing for the fifth time." Sophie crossed her arms, exasperated.

Maisy leaned against the bathroom door frame. "I'm texting with Brooks right now, and told him you and Rex have an official date."

"Oh? And what'd he say?"

"He said to tell you to be careful around Rex."

I didn't quite know what to make of it, but the door buzzer rang. "He's here. Okay, final outfit?"

"Yes!" They both yelled.

"I'll be right down," I spoke into the speaker for Rex to hear. He replied, "Okay."

"Now go on and have a great time, and text us if you're staying overnight so we don't worry about you." Sophie held out my toothbrush just in case. It hadn't dawned on me that this date might turn into an all-nighter in Rex's bed.

"And do be careful," Maisy warned, the tables turning.

"Who's acting the mother now?" I smirked and wrapped a black shawl around my shoulders. "Besides, with the fact that you're texting both Brooks and Archer, maybe I should be concerned about *you*? These are older men and you're still young—"

"I'm fine. And I'm not texting Archer anymore, just Brooks. He's asked me out to dinner. I told him maybe next week after midterms."

"Brooks?" I arched a brow, and the buzzer buzzed again.

"Your impatient man waits for you. Go. We'll talk about this tomorrow." She shooed me away.

"Fine. Love you." I closed the apartment door behind me and stopped, taking in a deep breath. As elegantly as I could, I treaded down the steps in my black patent heels until Rex appeared outside the window of the door, eyeing me up and down.

"My God, I'm not sure I can be seen with you in public tonight," he addressed me as he held the door open.

My heart dropped. "I knew it. I'll go back up and change."

"Are you kidding?" He pulled me back and closed the door, eyeing my cleavage. "You're stunning, lady in red. The problem is, I'll be a walking hard-on all night, not to mention have to hold myself back from knocking out every man who dares stare at you."

I sputtered a laugh, relieved at his comments. He held out his elbow for me and walked me to the car, and I walked a little taller next to him.

My confidence soared. I leaned in and whispered, "I'm wearing red lacy panties, by the way." His jaw set, and he growled.

As the driver held open the door for us, Rex's mouth descended on me, warming me, taking away all my nerves, replacing them with excitement for the adventures to come with him.

# 16

# 20K TO STOP

## REX

"*I*sn't this like the fourth date you've been on this month with Chelsea? That has to be a record for you," Pearl's shit-eating grin irritated me, which was probably how she planned it. I ignored her.

"She said she misses home and wants to go dancing at a country club where a friend of hers is a DJ tonight. I don't know. Are you sure about this?" I worried; my type of country club in high society didn't typically involve cowboys.

I stood in front of the bathroom mirror of my executive corner office. Pearl glanced over my shoulder at the clothes I had her order for me for this occasion. But Wranglers, flannel shirts, and cowboy boots? They weren't usually my style.

"Oh yes, trust me. You'll fit right in." She giggled on her way out.

"Glad my dating life amuses you. But I draw the line at wearing the cowboy hat." I smirked and tossed the hat back into the box. Shit, the lengths I went to for Chelsea…

But, if I was honest with myself, I hadn't tired of her yet, which surprised me. Most women bored me on or right after the first date.

She dazzled my friends, too. That night at the wine bar, she was the lady in red no one could take their eyes off of. Xander, Brody, Gage all met us there and I couldn't help but puff out my chest with her on my arm. She kept up with the conversation, mesmerizing everyone with her bright smile, and seemed to fit in well with us.

How perfectly she fit with me later that night, too, in the bed of the penthouse suite I'd rented at the hotel next to the bar.

On two other dates, I wined and dined her at some of New York's exclusive and finest restaurants and took her to fancy hotels after. I adjusted myself thinking of those nights in bed with her. Woke up each of the next mornings invigorated, as if the small town girl breezed into the city and took my life hostage somehow.

I wasn't complaining, and she'd better be impressed with me and my lifestyle by now.

I enjoyed showing her the finer side of life, watching her eyes grow wide at it all. She was suddenly occupying too many of my thoughts. Something I grew used to, especially for my plan to work.

After haggling with my lawyers about every detail, I finally had a prenup and a marriage contract. I even had a huge 6-carat Tiffany ring picked out. Now, I just needed to find the right time to proposition her with the idea of marrying me.

I'd had everything set, but kept putting it off. Part of it was nerves—it wasn't everyday I asked a woman to marry me for convenience and give me what I wanted. But I wasn't a total asshole; I had a sweet deal etched out for Chelsea in this marriage, too. She'd walk away with plenty once it was over.

Over...I'd probably miss her when she was gone, but surely I'd move on. Return to my playboy lifestyle and see this as nothing but an interesting experiment on the lengths I'd go to get everything I wanted.

Now, I'd bide my time, waiting for the right moment to

bring it up. My business instincts for negotiation in my real estate deals were usually on point, but this...with Chelsea...I couldn't get a feel yet for the right time to close this deal.

PEARL WAS RIGHT. My outfit blended well at the country bar among the other men. The only difference between me and them, was I probably could buy the bar, pay each man and woman in here at least a year's salary, and call it a day without blinking an eye.

I scanned the crowded bar for Chelsea, since she and her friends arrived earlier for trivia. I wasn't about to sit in for that, and told them I'd meet up later, but I didn't count on Brooks being here. He laughed at me as I approached.

"Well Goddamn, Rex—Buchanan Energy already owns the East. Are you looking to win the West, too?" He snickered.

"Yeah, keep laughing asshat. At least I tried to fit in." Although eyeing his casual jeans and black t-shirt, I was a little jealous. "What are you doing here?"

"I'm here with Maisy." He took a swig of his beer.

"Does that mean you have no designs on Chelsea?"

"She's all about you, my friend. You're *all* she could talk about during trivia." He rolled his eyes and took a swig of his beer.

Smiling inwardly, I could strike Brooks off my list of competitors for Chelsea's affection. "Look, I like her, and how many women have I said that about or gone to bed with more than once?"

He studied my face for a moment. "You serious about her?"

"Yeah. So can we put our friendship back on track then? No hard feelings?"

"Hell, Rex, you and I have a history between business and play. Not going to throw that away over a pair of sisters."

"You and Maisy—?"

"We're just friends. She's a bit younger than most women I date. But I like her. A lot. And, um…she's a virgin." He smiled sheepishly. My eyebrows shot up to my hairline at that news. "Yeah, so I'm not going to be that asshole who takes it from her unless it means something. I'm taking this one slow."

I nodded, completely understanding. "And how's Archer?"

He blew out air while shaking his head. "Back to the same old. Brianne's got him in her claws, and already playing her games with him. Fucking bitch."

"Do you want me to hire someone to off her?" I joked, sort of, and Brooks laughed and slapped my back. I hated to see what this awful woman had done to one of my friends. When she and Archer first met at a sustainable building materials convention, I wouldn't say it was love at first sight, but they started hot and fast. Little did Archer know then how toxic the woman was. We all could see it, but female attention blinded him.

"It's not a bad idea, but I think Archer is getting tired of her and starting to see he deserves better. I'll keep you posted." He lifted his chin, looking over my shoulder and I turned with a double take, finding Chelsea coming toward me looking hotter than hell.

Her tight jeans showed off curvy hips as she sashayed toward me. In a yellow and black flannel shirt with the arms ripped off, and tied tight above her waist showing off plenty of creamy skin at her midriff, she had my cock twitching. I had no idea how badly he wanted to ride a cowgirl.

Upon closer inspection, as she neared me, I realized she mustn't be wearing a bra. Her erect nipples on full display, I eyed-fucked her plenty. But my jaw set because probably so did every other man in the building.

"Rex!" All smiles, she threw her arms around me. I could

smell a sweet alcohol concoction on her breath. "I'm so glad you're here."

The song changed over to something slow, and she practically leapt out before I could wrap my arms around her. "Oh, I love this song. Come on, let's dance."

She dragged me out, and I was never so grateful for a slow song. This I could handle; my arms circled her waist, held her close, and we swayed to the music. Anything more, like a country two-step or line dancing, was beyond me. Archer was always the one with the dance moves among my friends.

"Mm. You feel so good, sexy-Rexy-poo."

"Been drinking already?" I asked, but knew the answer. Her half-lidded domes lazily gazed upon me, and her giggles were sweet but silly.

"I maybe had a few before you arrived. Oh, some shots, too, thanks to Brooks buying rounds for us."

I shot daggers from my eyes at Brooks, who grinned back. It seemed he had his hands full with Maisy, at least, who also appeared drunk and draped all over him on the dance floor.

"Wish you would have waited for me to arrive before having too many," I scowled.

"Why? Imma big girl, and I can drink without you." Her words slurred.

"When was the last time you were *this* shit-faced?"

"Hm. Years ago. I'm not usually a heavy drinker." She hiccuped.

"Just what I figured. Chelsea, this is still the city. Two drunk sisters can find themselves in some trouble with bad elements around every corner. This isn't Heart Hills, USA, where everyone knows your name." Just what I needed, Chelsea getting herself into trouble.

"Holly Creek, dammit. Learn the name of my hometown, will you?" She pouted and turned quiet.

Damn. Was this our first argument, right here in the middle

of the dance floor, swaying to some song about making love in a hayfield?

"Sorry," I mumbled. There weren't many women I'd ever had to apologize to.

"I've worked so hard, Rex, and just wanted to have a night to let loose, you know?" Her jade-colored irises set all innocent-like upon me. It worked, and I gave in.

"Fine. I'm here now, so I'll watch over you. Have all the drinks you want, on me."

"Yippee." She jumped up on me, locking her ankles behind my back. I twirled her around at first, laughing and capturing her mouth with mine. Then I carried her off the dance floor, back to where Maisy and Brooks sat at a table.

After a few more drinks—watered down as I ordered them from the bartender—and playing a round of darts and a game of pool, I went for the bathroom. Upon returning, Maisy was half asleep, swaying with Brooks on the dance floor again, but I couldn't find Chelsea anywhere.

I finally spotted her in a flash of yellow flannel, heading out the smoking door with someone. I rushed out after them and found it was the DJ smoking and Chelsea shivering next to her in the crisp autumn night air.

I raised an eyebrow at them. "Hey. There you are."

"Oh, Suz, this is Rex, my handsome date," Chelsea slurred her words and hooked elbows with me. The DJ exhaled her smoke in the opposite direction from me. Good thing, because I couldn't stand smoke.

"Hi, Rex. I've heard a lot about you." Suz held out her hand.

"How long have you been smoking?" I asked, ignoring the pleasantries.

"Um..." Her eyes shifted between me and Chelsea.

"Because smoking kills half of the users who don't quit, in case you didn't know. Have you ever tried to quit?" I continued my line of discussion, one I was familiar with, having been in it with dozens of other people, making it my life's mission to get people to quit.

Chelsea pushed her locks behind one ear. "Rex, sweetie, maybe this isn't the time or the place—"

"Would next year be better? Another year of Suz sucking on cancer sticks, and reducing her lifespan? How many packs do you smoke a day?"

Chelsea gasped, and Suz appeared incredulous.

"None of your business, man. Chelsea, I'll see you later." She started toward the door, but I had something that would stop her.

"Ten thousands dollars is yours if you quit in the next thirty days," I called out. She stopped in her tracks, half-turned and scowled at me.

"What?"

"You heard me. I'll pay you ten thousand dollars if you quit. Hell, make it twenty." I stood my ground.

She stomped back to me. "I won't stop just because you throw money at me."

"Are you sure about that? Could you use twenty thou to pay off your bills, to buy new equipment for your DJ business? Hell, quit working other jobs and try doing DJ gigs full-time?" I crossed my arms, and watched her face change to realize my offer would mean a world of difference to her.

She scoffed. "What's the catch?"

"Nothing. It's the honor system. I'll meet you right back here in thirty days and if you tell me you've quit smoking, I'll shell out twenty thousand in cash." I took out my phone and brought up my calendar.

"I could come back and tell you I stopped just for the money. How would you know?"

"The point is," I shook my head. "*You'll* know. Do you believe in karma?"

"Rex, what are you doing?" Chelsea asked.

"I spent years with my father smoking, and he ended up with lung cancer. The day he died, he still smoked. I made a vow to help any smokers who came within ten feet of me stop smoking. So, Suz, yes or no? Take me up on my offer—it only comes around once."

She inhaled in and out slowly and brushed her purple hair back with one hand. "Yeah. Okay. Fine."

"Good." I punched in the details into my calendar and handed her a card from my wallet. "Here's a help center I fund in Manhattan if you need resources to help you quit. See you in thirty days." I took Chelsea's hand and led her back inside and didn't stop until we were out the front door.

"You-you can't just go around offering people money to quit smoking," she exclaimed.

"Sure can. Just did." I texted my driver to come get us. "I do it all the time. Since watching my dad die slowly for a few years after his diagnosis. No amount of money could pay him to stop, despite having the best medical care and treatments. He was a good man, just had this one vice he could never shake."

"I'm so sorry about your dad." Her hand flew to her heart. "How many people have you helped like this?"

I shrugged, never kept count. "Made the offer a few dozen times. Smoking is hard to quit, though. Only half a dozen ever came back thirty days later saying they quit. But at least that's half a dozen I saved."

"My God. Rex, you have a good heart, you know that?"

I snorted. "Yeah."

"You do. Maybe other people don't see it, but…I do." She stood on tiptoes and kissed my mouth. Just when I went to circle my arms around her, she backed off quickly.

Her hand flew to her mouth. "Oh, no."

"Uh-oh," I winced, observing her creamy skin turn green. Sure enough, she bent over the bushes and hurled the contents of her stomach. I rubbed her back and held her hair.

"Take me home. I don't feel good," she cried.

"No. I'm taking you to my place so I can take care of you."

"Your place?" She whispered.

"Yeah, my place." Rarely did I have women over to my place. I didn't like them invading my space. But with Chelsea, she turned my universe upside down.

# 17

# APOCALYPTIC HEART

## CHELSEA

*N*ow I knew what I'd look like if the zombie apocalypse ever occurred. "This is amazing. Great job!" I complimented the hair and makeup artist. I hardly recognized myself, between the makeup and fake blood covering every inch of my skin and hands, and the streaks of black and silver they painted into my hair.

When Sophie and Maisy were also all made up, we took photos together. Complete with clothes we got from a salvation shop that we dirtied up and ripped to shreds, we were ready for our roles tonight.

"I can't believe how perfect our costumes turned out. Sophie, thanks so much for getting us into this," I said.

"Of course. I score an entry into the city's largest ball for a good cause and you think I'm not taking my two besties with me?" She cackled, already trying out a zombie-like laugh that sounded more like a witch.

The annual Zombie Ball was all we heard about for the past week as soon as Sophie came home from classes and told us about it. Through her friends in the drama club, she found out they needed zombie extras to walk around the ball and interact with the guests, pose for photos, and provide flavor for the event. This wasn't on my bucket list, but I added dressing as a zombie as an addendum at the bottom.

We mingled at the huge ball held at the Waterfront, where a thousand guests were expected.

"This is wild," Sophie shouted above the music. "There's food, alcohol, dancing with a live band, and a silent auction of expensive art. It's all for a great cause."

She pointed to a huge sign reading, "Zombie Ball: New York's Halloween Bash to Fight Lung Cancer." I skimmed the rest of the sign and when I got to the bottom, I noticed the fine print. A little important detail that might have been nice to know. The Buchanan Energy Group and Buchanan Family sponsored the event.

My hand flew to my mouth. Rex hadn't mentioned anything about this, and surely it'd be an important event to him since his father passed away from this horrible disease. I looked all around me, but with the masses of people dressed in costumes there was no way I'd find him if he was here. I resorted to texting him.

*Chelsea: Are you at the Zombie Ball? I am.*

I thought I'd mentioned to Rex that I'd be working here with the girls, but maybe I hadn't. It'd been a busy week for both of us and we'd had little time to get together or talk, other than a few texts here and there. After only a handful of dates, I felt like I was ready for more, but sometimes there still seemed to be a distance between us. We might go a few days without chatting, then suddenly he'd want to talk and get together—wait.

Was I just a booty call for him?

I shook off the question. No, it couldn't be. Not with the way Rex looked into my eyes, held me in bed, and talked about things each time after we had sex. And the way he took care of me after I got drunk that one night, taking me to his apartment and admitting how special I must be since he allowed me there.

Okay, so things were casual between us, but my heart started believing there could be something more growing and only one direction we were headed.

We looked over the art pieces up for auction. A painting of the Eiffel Tower in Paris in particular caught my eyes. While Sophie and Maisy chatted about their party strategy for mingling as zombies, I waited for a return text from Rex that never came.

Suddenly, a woman carrying a walkie talkie in one hand and a tablet in the other rushed up to us. "Ladies, we need zombies over where the photographer's setup to pose with the guests. Right over there, go on. Hurry." She pointed with the antenna of the radio.

We all shrugged and rushed to the platform where the photo opportunities took place. For over an hour, under the hot lights, we must have greeted hundreds of guests and posed until our facial muscles spasmed from all the smiles.

We took turns taking breaks, so Sophie and Maisy left briefly for the bathroom and to scrounge up food and drinks for us. I waited for the next couple in line for photos to step forward when a deep voice I knew well hit my eardrums.

Rex appeared with a woman on his arm for the photo. My jaw hit the floor when I recognized the woman from the party out at the Hamptons. I'd never be able to pull off her all-black leather skin tight ensemble on her perfectly tall model-like figure. With a tail and black ears poking out of her big blonde hair, she dressed up as a cat woman.

He wasn't really in costume, but wore a sharp black suit with a black t-shirt underneath. Handsome as ever with his hair slicked back, his blue eyes crinkled in the corners when he laughed at something the woman said.

What was this? Had he been stepping out on me the entire time? I had no one to blame, though. It wasn't like we'd ever talked about dating exclusively. But the apocalypse going on in my heart was fierce.

The photographer snapped his fingers at me, taking me out of the trance of devastation. "Hello-o. Zombie number three—" that was me. "Could you step into the photo frame, please?"

The photographer's assistant posed us all with the blonde woman standing in front of Rex, her back to his chest, his hand at her elbow and his other at her hip. And me? I was posed at her side with my arms in the air, my hands like claws, looking like I'd attack and eat her any minute. Little did they know, my claws really were out, ready to gouge her eyes and to pounce on Rex, the dark-suited bastard.

I should run far away from him, protect my heart, and forget this madness. I never wanted a relationship anyway, only to enjoy the city and work on the opportunity with the deli. But for some reason, Rex crashed into my life unexpectedly.

I froze to the spot, never straying my eyes off of him. The photographer snapped a few photos, the flash bulbs burning the memory of his hand gripping her hip into my skull. "Okay, now, Mr. Buchanan, get a little closer to your date," he said. "How about you two face each other? Squeeze in, that's it. Now put your arms around her. Good, and look into each other's eyes."

As they settled into the new pose, a lump formed in my throat at the sight of them together and his eyes on her. A sound came out of me I didn't recognize, a shriek or cry or something guttural and painful emanating from my heart.

Rex's eyes shifted to mine and locked there. His forehead furrowed. "Chelsea?"

I backed up, shaking my head, unbelieving this horrible moment, but tripped over one of the photographers' lights. It crashed to the ground, and I jumped out of the way, narrowly missing the sparks from the broken bulb that set the nearby curtain of the stage on fire.

Flames sprouted quickly and women screamed, people ran,

and someone yelled "Fire!" Amid the chaos, I couldn't move, until Rex abandoned his date and grabbed me by the elbow, leading me away from it all.

I was too blinded with rage, embarrassment, and heartache to resist. Alarms blared, and he led me through the service doors, through the kitchen, and out to an alley behind the building. Sirens of fire engines approached and it wasn't until he grabbed both my arms, with my back against the brick exterior wall of the building, that I came to my senses.

"Chelsea? Are you okay?" He sort of shook me, leaning down to my eye level, his stare intense, like he was trying to assess the damage he'd done to me. But how could he read into me with the anger flashing through my eyes?

"Let me go. I'm fine." I yelled and yanked out of his grasp. "Why don't you go check on your other girlfriend? Or the dozen other women you string along inside, for all I know, you...you playboy."

I never mastered the art of arguing with someone, preferring to kill them with kindness instead, but this...with him? Kindness wouldn't do.

"You don't know what the fuck you're talking about. Marlena is a family friend. My mother puts on this event. Marlena's mother helps her with it, and they asked that I bring her here."

"Why didn't you tell me you were going to be here with her?"

"Frankly, it'd been a busy week, and I wasn't even planning to attend, but pressure from my mom... Shit. You don't know my mother, but she's a pain in my ass sometimes."

"But the way the photographer was posing you, so—so intimately."

"You're right. I should have kept her at arm's length, but I just wanted the photo op done, make a quick appearance for

Mom's sake, and get the hell out of here. I planned to call you after to see if we could get together tonight."

He paced away, scrubbing a hand through his hair. "Jeez. And now, the entire event is up in flames."

My heart sank and tears welled up. I dabbed at them to keep from ruining my makeup. "Because of me."

He glared at me as his phone rang in his pocket and he took it out. "Shit. It's Mom. Hello?" He stepped to the side to talk. I brought out my phone and texted Maisy.

*Chelsea: Are you two okay?*

*Maisy: Yes, we're outside in front of the building. Where are you?*

I had no idea where I was. Stuck somewhere between wanting to fix this with Rex, and wanting to run away, all the way back to Holly Creek.

*Chelsea: I'm with Rex. I'll be home later.*

He finished his call, tucked his phone into his pocket. With his back to me, he sighed heavily with his hands on his hips. "Mom needs me inside to help assess the damage. The sprinkler system finally turned on and demolished all the decorations, the band instruments, thousands of dollars in damages to the hotel. Several people helped carryout the artwork before it got ruined, but the fundraiser is over."

"It's all my fault. I ruined this for you and your family, and it was supposed to be in your father's honor. I swear I'll pay back every penny—"

"Hey, hey. Stop." He rushed back to me and placed his hands on my shoulders. "It's only money and we always pay for event insurance. Besides, no one will know it was you."

I sputtered, crying, dabbing at my tears again. "You knew who I was, even under all this makeup."

"It was your beguiling green eyes. I'm pretty sure I would find you anywhere in a crowded room no matter what you were wearing."

My heart surged back to life. "You were easy to pick out, with no costume."

"I had a costume." He pulled out a black mask from his jacket pocket and held it up to his eyes.

A chuckle rumbled in my chest, even though I didn't much feel like smiling yet. "A bat man? Actually, it suits you, being a billionaire and all. And I guess you were a hero saving me from the fire...and protecting me from being named the one responsible for all of this mess."

"I'm partly responsible, too, because I suck at relationships and being a boyfriend. If I were better at it, I'd have brought you with me tonight, and said screw off to Mom about Marlena."

"Wait. Could you rewind a little? Boyfriend? Relationship?" My eyebrows arched at him.

"Uh, yeah. I've been meaning to talk to you about that. Look, it's going to be a long night with Mom dealing with this. So, tell you what. Come over to my place tomorrow night, and I'll cook us dinner."

"You cook?"

"I can heat things up in the kitchen." The corner of his mouth lifted.

"Hm. This I have to see. I'll bring dessert. Or...I can cook us breakfast the next morning." My coy smile was back, ready to be with Rex again, ready to forget this whole ordeal and put this night behind us.

"How about both?"

"Hm. Tough negotiator," I quipped. A strange look crossed his face I hadn't noticed before.

"Yeah, um, so I'll send my driver to pick you up about seven. Okay?"

I nodded, and he brought me into his chest for a hug. "I really am sorry, Rex."

"Me, too." His hand threaded through my hair, pulling gently back so my head lifted to him. And finally, our lips reunited in soft, sweet kisses. I wanted more, but knew for tonight, this had to be enough.

When he pulled away, I reached up and removed my makeup smudges from his lips and chin. "For the record, I've never been a fan of Halloween, and tonight just solidified that once and for all," I chuckled. "Christmas is my favorite holiday, and it'll be here before we know it. What?"

His face scrunched up at what I said. "It's just...Christmas hasn't been my favorite time of year for a while." His phone broke into the conversation before he could expand upon that.

He peeked at the caller id and sighed. "It's Mom again. I have to go. Will you be okay to get home?"

"Yes, I'll catch up with Maisy and Sophie."

"Okay. See you tomorrow night, at seven." He pecked the top of my head and rushed off, leaving me to worry about the bomb he just dropped.

What was happening right now? My...boyfriend...hated Christmas? Coming from Holly Creek, where everything revolved around the beloved holiday, that just wouldn't do. Sounded like I needed to write a new bucket list for Rex with all the things to make him love Christmas again.

# 18

# UP TO THE ROOFTOP

## REX

*I* paced when nervous, and tonight was no exception. I also cut myself shaving, broke out in a cold sweat, and almost burned my hand taking the baked brie out of the oven for our appetizer. But I'd chilled the champagne and everything was ready.

A glass of Macallan and a few deep breaths were in order before Chelsea arrived in about half an hour.

What was I so worried about? Oh, yeah. Ending my playboy days, committing to one woman, was kind of a big deal. Presenting her with a proposition for marriage was enormous.

With glass in hand, I strolled over to my penthouse windows, taking in the view, one of the best in New York. I could point out every building I owned through the glass. This was my world, and hopefully, it might become Chelsea's, too. For a little while, at least.

I patted the little box in my pocket. She couldn't possibly say no to the deal I fashioned. She'd have everything she wanted. Like—

A knock at my door interrupted my worries. Glancing at my watch, it was early; it couldn't be Chelsea arriving yet. I peeked through the peephole, surprised to find my neighbor Stanley there. With only two penthouse apartments on this floor, he had the other.

"Hey, come in. I haven't seen you in a while." I opened the door and welcomed the TV producer. "Want a drink?"

"Sure, thanks. I just came by to tell you I'm listing my apartment. I'm retiring in January and moving to Florida."

"No shit? Congratulations then." I crossed the room to my bar and poured him a glass of Macallan, too. He took it and we clinked glasses, strolling over to the window.

"Thanks. I'll miss this place, and I'll give proper notice to your management company."

I'd be sad to lose him as my long-time tenant. His hair had whitened over the years, but he appeared virile at his old age. I wished him well.

"How's the Morning City Show?"

He'd produced the city's number one morning TV program for years and won a few daytime Emmy's that he showed off in a glass curio cabinet on display in his entryway.

"Terrible. The boss said last minute he wants us to add cooking segments leading into Thanksgiving and Christmas, featuring comfort food, hoping to earn some ratings back. It's a pain in my neck that I didn't need this close to retirement. I already interviewed a dozen chefs and none of them were what I was looking for. I'm running out of time as the segments are supposed to start next week."

"What kind of chef?"

"Any kind, at this point. The segments take planning and preparation, and it needs to happen now." He appeared disheartened as he swallowed down half the drink, and suddenly, I knew who he should interview.

"Say, I know someone who would be perfect for the show. Chelsea Calhoun."

"Never heard of her. Where does she chef at?"

"First, let me show you this." I pulled up Chelsea's social media profile for Sun-Up Deli and played the video she did for peach pie.

"Look at her." Stanley practically tore the phone from my hands. "She's bright, happy, plays to the camera well. Perfect for the Morning Show. But can she really cook?"

"I wouldn't recommend her to you if she couldn't. Trust me, Stan, she's the woman for the job. You'd be foolish to not talk to her." I glanced at the time; she'd be here any minute, and I didn't want my evening plans disrupted by him. "Stop by Sun-Up Deli in the Buchanan building on Monday and speak to her yourself."

"Okay, I just might. Hey, thanks for this." He emptied his glass, handed it to me, and I set it in the sink on the way with him to the door. "Catch you soon."

"Oh, Stanley? If possible, don't mention that I referred her or we talked. If you like her, hire her on her own merits. Really, she deserves an opportunity like this."

"Sure thing. Talk soon."

How amazing it would be for Chelsea? And it could fit well into my plans. If she earned a regular spot on the show, and opened her eyes to more that she could do with her talents, maybe she'd let go of the deli. Hell, I could see it now, an entire brand built around Chelsea with cooking shows, cookbooks, online sales. I'd be happy to find her an agent and hire a PR firm and an expert consultant on these things. Anything to help her be the best in the business. I mean, if we were going to be husband and wife, why wouldn't I support her in her endeavors any way I could?

My mind raced with this turn of events until the knock came at the door. I'd keep this under wraps and hope Stanley reached out to her. Right now, I had a woman to convince to marry me.

I opened the door, and as always, the sight of her jump-started my heart. "Hello, sweetness. Come here."

She yelped as I picked her up and carried her through. Might as well get into practice now for carrying her over the threshold. Jeez. Who had I become, thinking about all this marriage stuff? If someone had told me a year ago that I would think of getting married, I would have laughed my ass off.

In her presence now, all my worries washed away seeing the bold smile split her face. Yeah, something about this felt right. I was definitely getting everything I wanted tonight. I set her down, and she removed her coat. Not wasting time in asserting myself, I claimed her lips.

She moaned and lifted her leg on me as I planted kisses across her bare collar bone thanks to a knockout red off-the-shoulder sweater she wore. "Should we skip dinner and get right to dessert?" She asked.

"Tempting, but no. I have plans for us tonight." I reluctantly put a pause on the kisses and took her coat and bag and hung them up. "Come with me."

She took my hand and laughed, but stopped when something caught her eye. "Hold up. What's this? Is that—the Eiffel Tower painting from the auction last night?"

The oversized oil painting was back in my home, thankfully one of few pieces not wrecked by the melee at the Zombie Ball. "Yes. It's mine, but I donated it to the auction. Now it's back."

"It's beautiful. One of my favorite things they had there."

"Really? It's yours. A gift from me."

Her jaw dropped. "What? Just like that? You're giving me a painting? I can't take that."

"Why not?"

"For starters, I have nowhere to hang it. I live on a couch right now."

"That won't always be the case. I'll, um, hold on to it for you until you're ready."

"Rex, I don't know what it cost you, but it's too expensive of a gift."

"Hey, you don't need to worry about me and money. I have it, I make it, I invest it, I spend it. If I want to give a beautiful woman something special, I will, no matter how much you protest."

Her hands massaged her temples. "Sorry. Sometimes it gets a little overwhelming how we come from two different worlds. I'm used to scraping by, and the simple things in life. I think the last thing a man ever bought me was a salad."

I snorted. She deserved more, better, and I was the man about to give her everything. "Let's make a deal. You don't complain when I buy you something."

"Fine, it's just I have nothing to give you in return. I mean, what do you give the man who has everything?"

"That's easy." I wrapped my arms around her and kissed her forehead. "Give me your time. Be patient with me because I'm a man, and as a species, we're known to be assholes now and again. And of course, pussy always makes a nice gift for any occasion, or just because."

"Rex." She burst out laughing at the last part, brightening my evening with her pearly teeth framed in red lipstick and a gorgeous curve to her lips.

"Add to that list—your sunshine. I could use more of it in my life."

"Really? Well, that could be arranged. I have plenty to give to the right man." She winked.

Would it be me? If she said yes, it would.

"Who knows? Maybe we'll hang it in our own place someday." I threw that out there, as it sounded like the exact sappy thing a hopeful man would say.

"*Our* own place?"

"Sure, I hope I'm not too presumptuous here as to where this might be headed." I took up her hand, lead her up the stairs, and felt her out with that question, just to be sure what page she was on.

"No. Not at all. Presume all you want."

That was a relief. With each step we took, landing at the top, I gained more confidence in the outcome for tonight. I stopped at the top of the stairs and I captured her lips again. The same jolt of electricity hit me, as it had every time we connected. Was it just me? Falling into this role with her seemed easy and comfortable.

I opened another door and was about to take her up a skinny flight of stairs to the roof, but she held back.

"I don't know where you're taking me, but I have something to tell you." A hint of worry crowded her voice.

"Oh, yeah?" I paused, hoping she'd make this fast because I suddenly I needed for her to see everything I had waiting for her.

"Rex, I called Uncle Doug today and told him I decided to stay here. I asked him to renew the lease. This is what I want more than anything, to make a good life and a good living running the deli. He agreed and said he'd call your office next week to arrange it."

What she wants more than anything? What about me? Would she want me in five minutes after I told her *my* grand plan for us?

I simply nodded toward the stairs. "Come on."

"Wait. There's something else I want to tell you."

"Okay." I cocked my head.

"These past couple months, getting to know you, have been crazy good. Unexpected. Since last night, I've been thinking about how I reacted seeing you with Marlena. I was so jealous, and I think that must mean...I'm falling for you," she ended in a whisper.

I broke out into a smile all over again and claimed her lips. Yes. Everything was falling into place. I had her on my hook.

We took the short flight of stairs, and, once we stepped outside onto the roof, the cold air hit us, but I was prepared. With a few clicks on my phone, the rooftop lit up with string lights everywhere, propane heaters turned on, and a snow machine at the base of the water tower above blew a light dusting of snow everywhere.

"Oh, my—what is this?" Her face, like a child's, captured the magic all around us as she took it all in. Exactly the look I was going for. But I didn't stop there. The rooftop was where Dad asked Mom for her hand in marriage. Surely it would work with Chelsea.

I led her down a path of rose petals to a table covered in white linen with a bouquet of red roses lit up by candlelight. As we got closer, in the middle of the table, a black velvet ring box became visible, and I reveled in her eyes growing wide at seeing it.

Now for the hardest part.

# 19

# THE GRAND PLAN

## REX

*C*helsea glanced around the rooftop. "What's going on, Rex? Is this what I think it is?"

I pulled out a chair for her to sit, and tucked her in, then sat myself across from her, laced my fingers over the folder on the table, and cleared my throat.

"This all started several years ago..." I paused and took a deep breath. "When my dad collapsed in Sun-Up Deli on Christmas Day. He was rushed to the hospital and passed away some days later."

"What?" Her face fell. "Uncle Doug never said anything. Why didn't you tell me?"

"It's difficult. Dad and his damn business and poker games and smoking...all of it took him away from Richard and I. When he had time for us, he was great. But it was too little. Christmas mornings had always been magical. Plenty of gifts, laughter, food, and fun. But he'd head to the deli with Doug and his cronies and play their poker game, Christmas Day be damned."

I still get pissed every time I thought about the end of his life and how it didn't have to be that way if he'd made different choices. He could have chosen to quit smoking. He could have spent more time with us over the year and in his final days.

"He was losing the battle with his cancer, and he should never have gone there that day. But they were like his extended family—and I resented all of them. Especially my—" I swallowed down the lump in my throat. "Especially my father."

She placed her hands over mine, and her mouth opened and closed a few times, like she struggled to find the right words to say. I continued on.

"I never wanted anything to do with Buchanan Energy, so I made my own way in real estate. Eventually, Dad told me how proud of me he was, making a name for myself in the city. Toward the end, we saw eye to on eye on several deals and I finally grew to respect him and his business advice more and more. But his damn refusal to give up his friendships and smoking, and not following doctor's orders, took him away from me too soon. Fucking stupid."

"I-I don't know what to say, but I'm here for you. I'm so glad you're telling me these things." Through her eyes, I could see the care there for me. It encouraged me to go on, revealing my deepest inner thoughts.

"After he passed, I couldn't walk into the Buchanan building or the deli without smelling smoke and getting physically ill over it all. It was a psychological response, I learned, and I've dealt with it with one of the best therapists in the city. But when Richard stepped down and our mother begged for me to take over, I had to face it and walk into the building every day. But, if I had my way, I'd tear down the entire building and start anew."

The pieces of the puzzle were starting to connect for her. "So the deli was not only the place of a harrowing incident when you were a boy, but also a reminder of the end of your father's life?"

I nodded, watching the color drain from her face.

"And that's everything? The actual reasons you can't walk into the deli without having an anxiety attack?"

I nodded again. "Everyone sees me as this rich playboy, when really I'm a total fucking mess inside. My therapist says I try to hide it and overcompensate by being a real egotistical prick. Ah fuck." I leaned forward, my elbows on the table, and massaged my forehead with my fingertips. "I can't believe I just told you all of this. Mom and Richard and Pearl are the only other people who know. You probably see me as weak now."

"No, I don't. I'm honored you feel you can trust me with this." She reached for my hands and took them away from my face, holding them on the table between us. "I see you, Rex. I see the scared little boy inside of you who loved his father immensely. Grief can do things to the ones left behind, I know. My family and I had our own things to work through after Dad passed, and mental health became so important for us to heal. We have so much in common, you and I. What can I do? I want to be there for you, so tell me what you need from me?"

I swallowed hard. This was it, and no time to back down now. "I do have something I need from you. Marry me."

She straightened in her chair, giving me a stare I couldn't read into.

"Rex, all of this is so…so sudden." She motioned around the roof. "I'm falling for you, yes, but I didn't expect something like this so soon."

"So you're saying no."

"I'm saying *maybe*, with time, it's a yes."

"That's not good enough. I *need* a firm yes, now. You see, to gain approval for my remodel plans of this building, the board of directors and my mom require me to settle down and get married."

She huffed with her brows arched. "Oh, so they're sick of your playboy ways?" Her hands left mine, and she stood. "Give me a minute here." She walked away, looking out at the lights, holding her sides. It took all my patience counting slowly to sixty before I approached her from behind.

"I want to remodel the lobby of the building. Remove all traces of the past and make it new and fresh. Make it something that future generations of Buchanans will be proud of."

She spun around. "Is that what you think you need in order to heal?"

I cocked my head at her. "Yeah, I think I do. Look." I took her by the hand, back to the table, and pulled out Archer's drawing. "Here's what the new lobby will be like when finished." I motioned here and there, pointing out where the new restaurants and shops will be, and talked about the unique sphere entrance. I stood back with a grin, admiring it like it'd be my greatest masterpiece when complete.

"I can understand that buildings need updating now and then. But—wait." She pointed a finger to where the Buchanan Energy sign sat on the concourse and traced a path to the deli on the corner, putting it all together. "My corner space looks different. Where's the deli on this plan?"

A sinking feeling overcame me, almost like a warning not to proceed, but I'd come this far. I retrieved the papers and spread them on the table. "About that, it won't exist, but marry me, Chelsea, and I'll give you anything else you want. In fact, I have some ideas I've drafted in this proposal."

"A proposal? This sounds more like a business deal, not a marriage proposal."

I displayed the prenup and marriage contract on the table.

"You'd never have to worry about money again, and your mother, too. I'll pay Doug handsomely for his deli and then some, and he can retire in style. For you…I'll give you *everything* you ever dreamed about. Culinary school, a trip to Paris to study with the best pastry chefs, and here in New York, your own restaurant, either in the new lobby of the building or anywhere else you'd like to open one."

She chewed her cheek and my shoulders dropped; she didn't look happy.

"So the only reason you want to marry is to get what you want?" Tears welled up in her eyes.

"Don't get me wrong. This is a very real marriage proposal. I've never felt about any woman the way I do about you. Chelsea, please." I fumbled with the black box and took out the ring. Taking her left hand, I slid it on her ring finger. "Make me the happiest man in the world and marry me."

Her lips trembled, and the tears wouldn't stop. She looked down at the ring, at her shaking hand held in mine.

She was going to say yes. My victory was in sight.

Slowly, she brought her hand closer to her eyes and fingered the diamond.

She had to say yes. It's what I wanted. Her, the remodeled building, no trace of the past...I wanted it all.

My hope died, though, watching her remove the ring and put it into my hand. "Don't you know, Rex? All the money in the world can't buy you happiness."

She walked away and took the stairwell down.

"Chelsea, stop," I yelled. "Stop." But she didn't.

When I heard the door slam behind her, I screamed into the night as if every ounce of pain from my past released from my body. A swift breeze blew the papers and plans from the table, scattering them all over.

I stared at the ring in my palm that I paid handsomely for. But Chelsea was right. Money didn't buy me happiness. I ran to the edge of the rooftop and threw the ring off into the distance.

## 20

# PURE KARMA

## REX

*I* had instructed Pearl to leave me alone today, yet she knocked on the door and let herself in anyway.

"What part of Do Not Disturb do you need translated into smaller words?" I grumbled. I didn't bother to lift my head off the desk where'd I'd parked it since I arrived.

I should have stayed home, but there, I was reminded constantly of Chelsea's rejection. At least here at the office, I had that, *plus* Pearl's interruptions to see me through the day.

"Okay. First of all, unless you tell me what's going on, I can't help you." Her tone sounded motherly, but I wouldn't fall for it. "Are you hangry? Need a pastrami—"

"Fuck no. Get out," I yelled, my heart lurching in pain at the mere mention of the sandwich I loved...made by a woman I could have one day loved forever if she'd have taken me up on my offer.

*Loved?* Ouch. More pain in the centered in my chest. When would it stop? I needed a doctor.

"Rex, at some point, whatever this is will pass, and you have responsibilities here."

"No."

"But there's someone here—"

"No!"

Suddenly, I heard another pair of heels clicking into the room. "My, he really is a grumpy baby, isn't he? I don't know how you put up with him."

My head popped up. "Marlena? What the hell are you doing here?"

"Pearl, be a dear and leave us to chat." She motioned with her black designer clutch at my office door.

"Rex, I'll be at my desk if you need me." The glares shared between the two women indicated no love lost there.

"Finally, we're alone," Marlena smiled with a similar haughtiness Mom always displayed, and plucked down into an office chair.

I rubbed my eyes to get the meshed vision of my mother and her as one woman out of my brain. "What do you want?"

"I told you at the party in the Hamptons what I wanted. My trust fund. I have to marry before I turn thirty on Christmas Day, and it's already early November. I don't have much time, Rex."

Oh good. Another reason to hate Christmas. "Not interested. Please leave and find some other sap to marry you."

From her bag, Marlena produced her phone, swiped through some things and placed it before me. Seeing Chelsea in her zombie get up knocking over the lamp sent me reeling. "How'd you get this? Mom and I paid off the photographer to lose the photos."

"And I paid him more to give them to *me*." Her stupid grin made me physically ill.

"Doesn't matter. You can hardly tell who it is with all the makeup."

"Hm, true. Except that photos of the zombies that night before the fire, show three women having fun working the event all over their social media profiles. It only took me a few clicks to find out who Chelsea is, the woman you were more concerned about getting to safety when the fire broke out, and never gave one glance over your shoulder at me. But don't worry. I made it out just fine."

"So, a lamp got knocked over. The fire was an accident."

"That's odd. My recollection of events—along with the photographer's—told the police otherwise. They're very curious who this perpetrator is who purposely set the room ablaze. And it'll take one phone call to the police to have her arrested."

"You wouldn't." Evil bitch.

"To get what I want? Yes, I would. There's two hundred and fifty million dollars wasting away in a trust fund that I want. Now, you're going to marry me or I'll turn Chelsea in."

"Don't do this."

"From the look on your face, she obviously means a lot to you. So, marry me, or send her to jail. I'll need your choice by the morning because time is wasting and even a small wedding like ours will take time to plan."

She stood and marched to the door, hesitating only to give me a final warning in her glance.

Karma, that's what this was. Pure fucking karma. And I deserved it after what I did to Chelsea.

Begging for her hand in marriage so I could remodel a fucking building I hated? Who the hell did that?

Me. I did, and probably ripped her heart to pieces by the look on her face when she passed me the ring back.

My own heart was acting weird, all achey and twisted. It had to be the guilt of what I did eating away at me with every second that passed. And now Marlena's evil plan was my penance. My choice was obvious. There's no way I'd let her send Chelsea to jail.

# 21

# JUST A BUG

## CHELSEA

*a* severe headache started the moment I woke up Monday, and didn't stop for three days. "I should have stayed home," I grumbled to Annie after I yelled at one of my best sandwich makers in the middle of the lunch rush. That wasn't like me, but Rex's so-called proposal still weighed heavily.

"Then go home, sweetie. We'll be fine. You should rest, get rid of this bug you've had," Annie said, a worried, motherly nature in her tone. With her graying hair tucked under a net and her wire-rimmed glasses, she often reminded me of an old picture from a storybook of Old Mother Hubbard.

That'd been my excuse since Rex's so-called proposal—A bug. Telling anyone I had a bug immediately earned me sympathetic eyes, offers of soup, and reasons to rest. In my case, perfect excuses to roll into a ball on the couch and cry until I had no tears left.

Annie was right. I had no energy for this today, and I couldn't even get the energy up to bake something, which usually was my go-to on the rare occasions when life pulled me down.

I looked around at the employees here who'd been so good to me, working so well for me, they'd become like family. I'd asked a lot from them as we grew fast this fall, serving more and more customers, and they had to work harder than the days when Uncle Doug ran things. But I wouldn't be any good to them unless I took time away to sort myself out.

"You're right. I think I will take the rest of today off. Call me if you need me." I patted Annie on the shoulder and waved goodbye to the rest of the crew as I took off my apron, pulled on my blue wool coat, and headed out the door.

My dark blue dress and coat matched my mood perfectly, especially given the overcast day. I sauntered outside, trying to decide what to do with myself because I couldn't face Rex yet. I wasn't ready to march into his office and give him a piece of my mind.

Marriage of convenience? Was he serious? That had to be worse than friends with benefits. Although if he'd asked for that I might have said yes as long as it was an exclusive arrangement. As friends, Rex might have woken up one day and realized he had fallen for me, too.

Lost in my heavy thoughts, several steps away from the deli, I stared at a sight that stopped me in my tracks—the familiar car parked on the curb of the concourse. Rex's car. His driver, Stephen, waved and smiled at me, leaning against the car, waiting. But I couldn't wave back, not upon watching Marlena and Rex walking out of the building together.

With their hands joined, she talked and gestured, but he was quiet. I could tell, even only knowing him a short time as I had, how sullen he appeared, eyes down, not cracking a smile, not twitching his lips at anything she said.

Stephen opened the back door for them and she got in. Then Rex spotted me and froze. He couldn't move either. His eyes were like sunken black dots with dark circles around them, his complexion paled, and he barely flatlined a smile.

With only a moment to linger, I couldn't breathe, shocked by the connection still so strong between us. Even now, it reached across the distance, closing the gap. How I longed to know his thoughts, to feel his touch, to kiss his lips, to figure out why he did this to me, but he shook his head and quickly entered the car.

"Bastard!" I muttered under my breath as they drove away, my ragged puffy clouds floating in the cold air.

He was with Marlena now? What, I turned him down so he took the *proposal* to the next available woman?

"Oh God. I can't do this."

Seeing Rex again stabbed me in my heart like a sharp knife, but seeing him with her twisted it in the wound. He meant more to me than I led him to believe.

I had wanted the deli, the man, everything. Now, I wanted nothing. I had told Uncle Doug to renew the lease, but if it meant running into Rex all the time, then forget about it. I'd never be able to get over him that way.

If not for my phone ringing, I might have stood there in that spot all day, contemplating my life since coming to New York. Was I any better or further ahead than the day I arrived?

Perhaps I should give up and go home, back to Holly Creek? Home, yes, my heart yearned to be home again.

The call went to voice mail, and finally I forced one foot in front of the other, walking and walking, until I reached Central Park. I hadn't spent much time here, and it definitely was on my bucket list to explore. Pleased I wore my flats, today was my lucky day to meander through the great park and think.

Before I could get too far into my thoughts, my phone rang again. I hissed and pulled it out. From a number I didn't recognize, I debated about not answering, but I noticed the last call was the same digits.

"Hello?" My voice wavered.

"Chelsea Calhoun? This is Stanley Proctor from the studios

of the Morning City Show. We came across your social media channel and checked out your deli. I wondered if you'd be interested in coming down to NYBC television studios to interview for a temporary position?"

"Um, what?"

The man sighed on the other end. "I said, this is—"

"Sorry, I heard all of it. What temporary position?" I hardly knew why I asked, especially when the pull of home called to me so strongly.

"We'd like to feature a segment about homestyle cooking and comfort food starting next week and running through Christmas. The segment would appear three times per week."

I blinked several times, as if that helped me process what the man said. This had to be some sort of crank call. "Right. Ha ha. Very funny. Whoever this is, hope you got a good laugh out of it."

I hung up and huffed on my way, only to be assaulted by the ring once again. Same number. I clicked on it. "Yes?"

"Hey look. I get it, it's not everyday a TV studio calls and thinks you're the perfect person for the job," Stanley's voice rushed in before I could speak. Did he say perfect person? "But I think you owe it to yourself to come down to the studio to do a screen test. I have openings at two or three this afternoon. What do you say?"

TV? Something like this never factored into my plans and dreams. It'd be a new adventure for sure. Something different. Something far away from Rex and the deli. And only temporary, while I figured out what to do with my life next.

"Sure. I don't know a thing about TV, though. I've never been in front of a camera."

"Are you kidding? I saw your daily lunch special videos on your social media channel. You were terrific. Trust me, whatever you don't know, I can teach you. So, two or three today?"

"Fine. Okay. Three. Oh, what should I wear?"

"That shouldn't even be a question considering your branding has been very consistent with bright dresses and flowers in your hair. See you this afternoon."

He clicked off, leaving me dumbfounded. He really did watch my social media. What was the old saying? A door closed, and a window opened, or something like that. With renewed vigor, I backtracked and headed to the apartment to pick out the brightest dress I had.

On the way, I called mom, anxious to share the news with someone, and I knew Maisy and Sophie were in classes.

"Flora's Diner." Colt's voice instantly brought a smile to my face.

"Baby brother! It's Chels."

"Hey, how's it going, big city girl?"

"It's going. How are things with you? How's the diner?"

"Things are...yeah." He sighed. Hm. Very ominous. "Listen, mom's at a dental appointment. And there's a lull right now before the lunch rush. I need to talk to you about something. Hang on."

I waited and could just picture him transferring the call into mom's office and shutting the door. Sure enough, when he clicked back onto the line, I heard the familiar squeak of her door hinges as he closed it. "You there?"

"I'm here. Tell me what's going on." Oh no. Things came in threes, Mom always said. I braced myself. First Rex, then the call with Stanley, and now...?

"Well, I've made a decision. I don't know how anyone will feel about it, but it's done. I've signed on the dotted line," Colt warned.

"Signed what? What did you do?"

"I've been on this health kick, you know, working out a lot. I talk with the owner, Trey of Treyner's Gym all the time. And as I've gotten to know him, he shared about his days as a Navy

Seal. And, I don't know. He's a cool guy. I like the way it sounds. So, I joined up."

I left the line sitting quiet for a moment, trying to understand what he just said. "You joined...the gym?"

"No. I joined the Navy. I report for duty on Valentine's Day."

I blinked back the tears, amazed I had any left by now. "Oh, Colt. Mom is going to flip. What if something happens to you?"

"What, like travel the world beyond Holly Creek? Get to learn some cool shit? Meet new people?"

"No, like be sent into a war zone...or something bad happens?"

He sighed. "You worry too much. I'll be fine. Besides, there's no sense talking me out of it now. I signed the contract with the devil. The military owns my soul for the next four years. Hey, how do you think I'll look with a high and tight haircut?" At least his good humor showed up about it. But Mom...once she heard his news, she'd be a basket case.

"When are you planning to tell Mom?"

"I figured at Thanksgiving, when you and Maisy come home for the weekend. Oh hey, I hear Mom's voice. Don't tell her, okay?" I heard the door to the office open, and he called to her. "Hey Mom, Chelsea's on the phone for you."

"Oh, gimme, gimme," Mom cried. "My Chelsea-Sunshine girl?"

"Hi, Mom. Miss you. Love you." I fought back more tears.

"Oh, darling, how are you?"

"I'm okay. First, how are you?" I bit back my tongue so hard to keep from blurting Colt's news.

"Wonderful. I just had my teeth cleaned. They're gleaming." I could see her running her tongue along the smooth ridges of her white teeth.

"Good. Well, you'll never believe this, but I'm going to interview this afternoon to be on television for the Morning City Show."

"Ah!" She screamed. "Our Chelsea is going to be on TV." She screamed again, sharing the news with whoever was in the diner at the time.

"It's a cooking segment, but I don't know yet for sure if I have the job or even know if I want to do it."

"Oh, honey. This is the best news I've had all day. Gives me a good feeling. You know what I think? You're young, so do the show, see where it leads. Maybe other opportunities come from it. You never know." My mother and her eternal basket of sunshine and optimism did my heart good to hear today.

"It is only temporary if I get it. I'll see how it goes."

"What's wrong, dear?" Her knack for sniffing out trouble remained keen. But I couldn't worry her about me, when she'd soon be worried enough about Colt.

"I just miss home."

"Oh, you'll be here soon for Thanksgiving. And you're always welcome home. Doug and Louisa will be up then, too, looking for a new place to live since they're moving here after the holidays."

"That's great news. Oh, Mom, I have to go. Talk soon, okay?"

"Love you, my sunshine girl."

As I clicked off and rounded the corner to the apartment, all of a sudden, the weight of my worlds pulled at me. My small town life versus my city life. I straddled them both, lingering in the middle, trying to figure out where I belonged.

# 22

# WANTS VS. NEEDS

## REX

For about the hundredth time, I watched every one of Chelsea's Morning City Show segments leading up to Thanksgiving, torturing my soul with her face and sunshine. This role on TV was designed for her. She. Was. Perfection.

When she laughed, I laughed, every time. She used all sorts of descriptive adjectives for her food, and my mouth watered for a morsel, *and the taste of her.* And when she talked about home, every fiber of my being wanted to exist in one with her.

A one-room home with a cozy bed was all I needed with Chelsea. We'd order food in, entertain each other, hold each other all night, make love—*Love!* In my mind, I said *I love you* to her every day since I fucked it all up, not realizing what I had until it was gone.

"What have I done?" I groaned. I was a complete ass to Chelsea and didn't deserve her.

Jeez, I'd turned into Archer—a brooding, pining prick. Now I had another thing to feel guilty about since I had little sympathy for Archer back when he went through his first breakup with Brianne. I owed him a huge apology.

There was no way around the predicament Marlena forced me into. I put her off as long as I could, but she threatened to call the police on Chelsea again unless we finally announced the news of our pending—and fake—marriage to our families on Thanksgiving day.

Fine. I deserved this. I'd take it as my punishment for what I did to Chelsea, but the guilt…oh the fucking guilt ate at me.

I clicked pause on the television screen and hauled up from my desk. Standing in front of Chelsea's frozen frame, I touched the back of my hand right on the cheek of the image of her. How desperate I felt to touch her flesh again, to kiss her lips, to be inside of her.

The woman did something to me and turned me into a mess. I was once a thriving playboy without a care in the world. Now? I was a pathetic fucking asshole.

There was only one way to resolve this, to ease my mind, or I'd go crazy. I needed a drink—*several* of them. Since Marlena, the evil witch, held me under her thumb, getting drunk was my coping mechanism.

I grabbed my coat and about rushed out of the office, but in my haste, I toppled over the model of the lobby redesign Archer and Brooks created. "Shit."

I placed the marble slab back on the table and stared at it long and hard. Then it hit me.

I flew to Pearl's desk, barking orders.

"Call Archer. Tell him to redesign the lobby to include the deli."

"Sure, you got it." She picked up the earpiece of the phone.

"Only tell him to do whatever he has to do to *double* the size." I yanked my coat on.

"Right."

"And tell him I'm footing the bill to remodel the entire deli for Chelsea. Anything she wants, she gets." I punched the elevator button.

"Okay."

"One more thing. Redo the deli lease in Chelsea's name, for twenty years, at the original lease price my dad set up with Doug. Get her to sign it."

"What? Really? Oh, okay. Only there's one problem."

Leave it to Pearl to throw a wrench into my plans. I faced her and sighed, irritated at her as usual.

"What?" I placed extra emphasis on the t.

"Your mother hasn't approved of your plans to remodel yet, has she?"

Shit. I grimaced. Soon though, when Marlena dragged me by a ball and chain to the altar, I'd get to remodel the lobby. And wasn't that what I wanted? I stepped onto the elevator, not at all sure anymore.

"Where are you going?" Pearl called.

"I have an important appointment to keep," I yelled as the door closed.

"Suz! You didn't let me down. You're here." My words slurred. I'd been sitting at the country bar since noon and now it was… five o'clock…maybe? I could barely read the digits on my phone.

"Yeah. Hi. I took up your offer. And here's a certificate from a program I completed at my community center to stop smoking." She proudly passed the sheet across the bar top to me.

"Awesome. That's so great. Come here." I gave her a hug, even though she was a little standoffish, but I didn't care. I was drunk.

*I lost Chelsea.*

I ruffled Suz's short spiky hair, and she looked pissed, but smiled anyway. Out of my breast pocket, I produced a thick envelope and handed it to her. "Here. Twenty thousand. Spend it wisely." I saluted Dad in Heaven with my drink, continuing my good deeds in my own way, happy that I saved another soul like Suz, adding years to her life. I slammed back whatever was left in the shot glass in front of me.

"Are...you okay?" She side-eyed me.

"Yeah, super. I lost the best woman that ever happened to me. But shit, you quit smoking. Let's celebrate. Bartender! This girl just quit smoking. Another round for the entire place on me."

Only a handful of people were here at this hour drinking, and they all cheered.

"Wait. Do you mean you lost Chelsea? What happened?" She took up the barstool and appeared genuinely interested.

"I fucked that up royally." My elbow landed on the bar and I dropped my head in my hand. "She'll never talk to me again. I'm such a stupid idiot." I hammered the bar with my other fist.

"Hey, knock that off or I'll kick you out," the bartender barked.

"Fine. Sorry."

"Um, listen. I'll be right back, okay? I have to make a call." Suz jumped off her barstool and rushed away.

"Sure. You come back and we'll have another round and celebrate you being smoke free. Another year of livin'. Woo. Here's to you." I put the shot glass to my lips but realized it was empty. "Bartender...another."

"Dude. I gotta cut you off," he said. Todd was on his name tag, or maybe Dodd. My eyes were too blurry to count the accurate number of Ds.

"I'll have a thousand bucks tip for you. Pour the damn round. It's only money. What do I care about it anymore? I don't care about anything. Without Chelsea, life means nothing. Nothing. I fucked it all up."

I sat at the bar a while, wallowing, and no further drinks came my way, no matter how much money I offered Dodd-with-morals. My mind recounted with blurred vision every second of that last night with Chelsea on the rooftop, listing every single thing I did wrong with her.

"Why does hindsight have to be such a bitch?" I rubbed my eyes. "What the hell was wrong with me?"

I knew what. I broke The Playboy Code #1. Never fall for a one-night stand. I did anyway. Chelsea blew into town and messed with my heart, and now I had nothing.

I hurt her for what? A fucking building. "Tear the whole Goddamn thing down," I shouted to no one. The bartender's face reddened. I hung my head and closed my eyes, drunk, pissed, sad.

With no sense of timing, how long I sat there a mystery, but suddenly someone appeared on the barstool next to me and slapped me on the back. I peeked over with one eye open, barely able to make out my brother. "Rich?"

"Hey. How are you doing? By the looks of it, not well." He grimaced.

"I didn't know this bar was your scene. You have cowboy boots on?"

"It's not. Someone named Suz called someone named Maisy, who then called Brooks to come get you. Only he was busy and passed the buck to me." He slapped my back again. "Guess we have some catching up to do. What's going on with you, dude?"

"I lost something."

"Sanity, dignity, money, what?"

"A woman."

"A woman?" He chuckled. "Bartender? I'm going to need two shots of your best whiskey for me just to get through this."

We waited for the drinks, and I licked my lips, watching him slam the first shot back, dying for another. "Okay, I'm ready. How did Rex Maximillion Buchanan, New York's biggest playboy, lose a woman?"

"Through my own stupidity. She's the most beautiful thing

to ever land in the city and I fucked it up. Mom said she'd let me remodel the building if I got married. So I propositioned Chelsea, and she turned me down."

"Propositioned? Oh-hoh." He howled. "What, like a fake marriage? Jeez, if Miriam found out it was fake, she'd lock you out of the building."

"That's the thing, though. It wasn't fake. I think I wanted it to be real. But it's too late now."

"Too late? You're giving up?"

"You didn't see the look on Chelsea's face."

"Come on. We're Buchanan's. We don't stop in the face of adversity. We keep going. If there's something we want—"

"We take it, I know, I know. That's what got me into trouble in the first place." I sighed and swayed, the bar spinning now. "But sometimes what we want isn't what we need."

Wow, that actually made a ton of sense to my drunken brain.

"You're really going deep, dude. How many drinks have you had tonight?" Rich was far too amused by my predicament to be of any help.

"Not enough." There would never be enough alcohol to fill the gaping hole in my heart.

"Look, if you really want her, don't give up."

Somehow his words both encouraged and saddened me at the same time. He was right, though. I shouldn't give up on her. She was the best thing that ever happened to me.

But...was I the best thing that ever happened to *her?*

# 23

# HER THANKSGIVING

## CHELSEA

The only thing I remembered about November, after Rex's fake proposal, was working night and day nonstop between the deli and the TV station. Who knew filming segments would be grueling? There were recipes to select, shop for, and try. Blocking on set and script writing, and coaching for how to present myself on camera. Wardrobe, makeup, and a dozen other things that needed my time and attention.

I took extra care to include homey touches or bits of history. Like how one of my ancestors created this recipe, or how many generations of my family had been cooking another recipe. Fans wrote in sharing theirs, and eventually we started featuring a few.

So much was involved in doing one five-minute segment per show, but oh, it proved more fun than I had anticipated. I fell in love with the temporary job.

Apparently, the station's upper management, and viewers loved it, too. By the second week of my appearances, ratings of the Morning City Show were doubled, and they asked me to appear every day, Monday through Friday, making it more like a full-time temporary job.

Being busy suited me fine, because it meant I didn't have extra time to think about Rex. I promoted Annie to watch over the deli when I wasn't there. I didn't have to be there as often to take the chance of running into the man who broke my heart. But there was still an empty hole there where Rex used to be, and something felt off-balance in my life because of it.

The day before Thanksgiving, during the last show for the week, I completed an extra long live segment, all about fixing the traditional turkey dinner with all the side dishes. I managed to pull it off without a hitch.

At the end of my segment, before the commercial break, the hosts and weather person crowded into my stage kitchen. We hadn't blocked this out in advance, so they took me by surprise.

Nancy Bauer, long-time hostess and anchor, talked first, her blue eyes and blonde hair perfection as she spoke into the camera. "Chelsea, you have been so fun to have on the set with us. Of course, we have an entire month with you still ahead where you'll showcase all new recipes for everything from Christmas cookies to pies and even what to do with leftover ham."

Raul James, the other main anchor of the show, exclaimed, "Yes, and my stomach is thankful for getting to taste test everything right here every day in December." Everyone laughed.

"But today, we have a special announcement that we think you'll be extra thankful for, Chelsea," Nancy shared. "Drumroll please."

"We have Julia Mason from the Tourism Board of New York City on hand with us today to present you with something," Raul announced.

"I'm so excited to be here today to announce that Sun-Up Deli has won the *Best* Deli Sandwich of New York City Contest.

Congratulations," Julia shook my hand, and camera flashes went off.

I stopped breathing, not believing this was happening to me. They'd have to call an EMT to jump start my heart soon. It was all too surreal and exciting. Confetti fell from the ceiling, hands clapped all around me, and horns blared as if it was some regal announcement. Julia handed me a golden trophy cup with Sun-Up Deli etched on it.

"Oh, my goodness. Thank you so, so much. This means the world to me," I gushed, and, finally, couldn't be prouder of my time here in New York City.

Raul closed the segment by saying, "Looks like you'll have something to be extra thankful for around your Thanksgiving dinner table at home this year. And now, a word from our sponsors."

"And cut," Stanley shouted, signaling the segment over and we were on commercial break. After everyone congratulated me again, the production assistants got to work cleaning up and clearing the set, and Julia made an appointment with me and her marketing team to do a photo shoot and mini-press tour the following week.

The whole day left me exhausted in a very good way, but one thing stuck with me. Being thankful tomorrow at home, in Holly Creek, with my family. Maisy and I were driving home tonight, and Sophie was coming with us as well, and we wanted to get an early start. I couldn't wait to hug Mom and Colt.

Stanley approached me as I tucked the huge trophy cup into my bag and prepared to leave. "Beautiful job today, Chelsea. Really outstanding work."

"Thank you so much. And if I haven't said it before, sincerely, thank you for hiring me," I gushed. I truly believed this show helped mend a little of my broken heart.

"Actually, we should thank Rex. He's the one who recommended you for the job. Ooh, wait." He hissed. "I think he said not to tell you that. But, hey. You're here, we love you and the job you're doing, and we think, because of you, our ratings are the highest ever. So as far as I'm concerned, I'd give Rex a gold medal," he laughed and clapped his hands.

"Oh. Sure." I hadn't realized the role Rex played in all of this. Learning this now, how did I feel about it?

"Listen, we'd like to talk about extending your contract."

Right when I believed this could have been the best day ever, it gets better. "You mean…"

"Beyond Christmas, into the New Year. We'll be reaching out to your agent to set up a time to work out details. But we're thinking at least 3 times per week and then perhaps some longer standalone specials six times per year around various holidays, or even traveling to different places in the region and exploring foods there. What's your initial reaction to that?" He grinned.

"You mean like a full half hour? Just me? I'd say yes. Amazing." This whole situation became better than *anything* I'd ever dreamed of before.

"Excellent. By the way, I told a friend in the publishing industry about you, and he's keeping his eye on you. So, just putting this out there, that you might want to start thinking about recipe and entertainment books." His arms spread open wider and wider. "Then, of course, that could lead to branding your own line of kitchen utensils, then cookery, and dishes—"

"Whew. Stop. You're making me dizzy. It all sounds amazing, but one step at a time, please. I'm just now getting my feet wet in television. Give me some time before I branch out into books and beyond," I laughed.

He stepped closer, crossed one arm on his chest, and pointed at me with the other hand. "Chelsea, I've been in business a long, long time. There's something you need to understand. Someone like you only comes along once in a blue moon. You have *star quality,* and I don't mean like a diva. I mean a person who can connect with people, reaching across the TV screen and drawing people in. Your ride to the top will be incredible, but it will be fast. I'd bet Chelsea Calhoun becomes a household name in one year."

"Stop. You're making me cry." I couldn't help but hug him. "Thank you, Stanley, for everything."

"You're very welcome. Go on and enjoy your holiday, and I'll see you next week."

Later, on the drive back to Holly Springs, Maisy and Sophie started calling me Star. I told them to stop. I certainly didn't have time to get a big head about this. In fact, I planned most of the weekend to pour through Mom's recipe boxes to create the perfect menus I'd be featuring all month in December. Mom already told me she couldn't wait to go through and share more stories about each recipe with me.

The girls quieted down at one point on the drive when we had a little ways to go. With nothing but time to think as I drove, my thoughts soon turned to what Stanley had said about Rex referring me to him for the job. If this is heading to a new career for me, then I guess I owed him some thanks if I ever saw him again.

If only Rex would have played it all differently, asked me because he truly wanted me to be his wife, not just wanted me to be part of his building plans...

If he didn't try to buy my answer to the question, *Marry me?* what would have happened with us then?

So many mistakes made on the way to what I believed could have eventually been true love. Problems too big to overcome now.

As if it were just yesterday that I took off his ring and walked away, my heart panged for him. To everyone else, he certainly embodied an egotistical billionaire, but for a brief moment, we shared something good and I saw right through his facade to the man underneath. He was mine, but it ended so stupidly, all too soon, and perhaps that was why I still longed for him, wondering if we could have been so great together.

About ten miles from home, a call came in from Colt. I clicked to answer hands-free and had him on speaker. "Hi. I suppose Mom asked you to call and check on us. We're almost there."

"Good, but that's not why I called," he said. "Listen, let's keep the news about me going into the Navy a secret for now."

"What this?" Maisy's eyes almost fell out of her sockets.

"Oh. I figured Chelsea would tell you," he said.

"Um. No, I didn't say a word. You told me not to, and that you'd be telling everyone together at Thanksgiving," I reminded him.

"Shit. You're right. But you know, we're all going to be together for the first time since you moved away. I don't want my news to ruin Mom's Thanksgiving."

I snorted, shaking my head, because this was so typical of him. On the other hand, he was right. This news could break her heart and have her crying all weekend. "Colt, do you need me to break the news to Mom gently for you?"

"No, not at all. I'll tell her, just not this weekend. She's been so excited to have all three of us under one roof for dinner."

"Three? Uh, Maisy? Did you forget to tell Mom that Sophie was coming home with us?" I tossed her a stern glance. She shrunk in her seat.

"Oh. Yeah, sorry. I've just been so busy writing papers for school and then with Brooks—"

"Okay, wait. Who the hell is Brooks, and is Sophie in the car with you?" Colt asked.

"Hi. I'm here." Sophie waved at the phone and laughed.

"Dang. Nice voice. What do you look like?"

"Colt!" I clicked off the call. In my rearview mirror, Sophie chuckled, but I warned. "He's too young for you."

Maisy guffawed. "Come on. There's only a two-year difference between them."

"Relax, sisters. I won't defile your little brother. I swear." Sophie winked at me. Oh, brother.

All warnings aside, my heart surged entering Holly Creek. Passing down Main Street, the family stores and eateries called forth so many memories. Of course, there was Flora's Diner, in its own brick building, standing so sturdy against time, never changing, and always welcoming with windows decorated for each holiday; right now, it featured fall leaves of all colors and shapes outlining the window frames.

Pulling into the driveway of our old farmhouse, just outside of town, Mom was there waiting for us. When we hugged, I finally felt home again.

# 24

# HIS THANKSGIVING

## REX

*S*tephen opened the car door for Marlena and she seated herself too close to me. I scoured the news on my phone and put more space between us, practically hugging my door.

"Hm. Not even a hello?" She asked.

"I'm marrying you so you can get your trust fund, not to become your best friend." I snapped. "By the way, there will be an ironclad prenup. You'll get your family money, but *none* of mine."

"Suits me fine. Since you're in a negotiating mood...what else should we hash out on this *pleasant* drive to your mother's house for Thanksgiving dinner?"

"No sex, obviously." There was only one woman I desired, and I blew that relationship out of the water. If I couldn't have Chelsea, then no sex for me for a while.

"What? You know there'll be all kinds of pressure on both sides for children," she countered, scowling at me with a snarled, red-stained lip.

"They won't be coming from me. You said marriage was all that was required to gain access to your trust fund. I see no need to perform beyond the minimum requirement. We divorce by July."

She shook her head and stared out the window. "Agreed, but it's *your* cheating ways and your very public display of an angry tirade at the country club that will cause me to run to a divorce lawyer."

I snorted at her requirement for *my* reputation to be the one soiled in all of this. Then again, what did I care? I'd be married, getting mother and the board of directors off my back, and remodeling Dad's building by then. I had nothing else to live for.

"Sure. I'll be the bad guy." A part I played very well, according to the hurtful look in Chelsea's eyes and her tears that night on the roof. "Anything else?"

"Public displays of affection—"

"Hell no." I drew the line there.

"But my father will expect us to be loving toward each other, even if it is an act. I already devised a plan that we've been secretly seeing each other and didn't want to announce our relationship until we knew for sure."

"Christ." I leaned my elbow on the window, and my forehead in my hand, weighing how little affection I could get away with. "Hold hands and smile and one kiss when we arrive and announce the engagement. One kiss during dinner. One kiss after. Hold hands while walking out to the car."

"Sufficient. But the kisses better linger and be damned convincing. We'll wed in a simple ceremony at the country club, inviting only close family and a few friends."

I hated having to discuss this when the woman I'd prefer to marry turned me down.

"We're here, sir," Stephen announced, eying me in the mirror. He's probably thinking what an idiot I was, and he'd be right.

"Thank fuck. Let's get the charade over with."

I let Stephen get the door for Marlena, and waited on the walkway for her. Once she stood by my side, I took her hand and plastered a smile on my face. I showed it to her, teeth and all. "Is this good enough for you?"

"Fuck you," she seethed, and planted her smile on as well as the front door flew open.

Mom shrieked. "Oh, look at the two lovebirds." Out from the house spilled her second husband, Sam Astor, and Marlena's parents.

Her mother, Theresa, approached right away and kissed my cheeks, probably leaving bright pink stains behind that would be tough to wipe off. "Oh, I always hoped you two would find your way to each other."

Her father, Henry, only gave me a curt nod. He had a permanent scowl on his face since the day I met him. Today, it appeared deeper set, if that was possible.

Suffering through dinner meant fumbling through answers to their twenty questions about our relationship, engagement, and early wedding plans. I'd say I over performed my role, being unusually jolly, nice, and rolling with it.

The entire time I thought of Chelsea and her "kill them with kindness" motto. She got the "kill them" part right.

As the evening wore on, I excused myself and wandered down the west wing to Dad's old study. Mom kept it as he last left it out of reverence for the love they shared. Dad may have had his faults, but his undying love and loyalty to Miriam wasn't one of them.

I could only hope someday, when—if—I married for real, I'd reach that level of love or higher with my wife. Jeez, there I went again, talking about marriage, when a year ago the idea of commitment would have made me sick to my stomach.

The door opened, and Mom walked in, closing it behind her. "I thought I might find you here. Turn on the fireplace, please."

As she coiled into a chair, her legs under her, she wrapped a blanket on top.

I fumbled with the gas logs and lighter, but eventually got it roaring, and sat on the wing chair next to her.

"I know you dating Marlena was originally my idea, but not like this," she started in on me.

"What do you mean?"

"Not this *fakery*." Her steely eyes stabbed me.

"Christ, isn't this what you wanted? Me married off as soon as possible before another gray hair grows on your head?"

"Mind your tone. I don't know where I went wrong with you and Richard."

I leaned forward with my elbows on my knees. "You did nothing wrong, except maybe you and Dad set the bar too high. Not everyone can find love like you had."

"I'm so disappointed in you, Rex. I asked you to open up your heart."

"I did, okay? With Doug's niece," I barked at her, letting the words fly out before I could stop them. I rubbed the back of my neck.

"Really? She seems like a lovely girl."

"Yeah, well, it...fell apart." I sauntered to the fireplace and leaned a hand on the mantel, wishing for time to speed up. "Because of my own stupidity."

"Well, maybe you could try again with her."

"I'm with..." I shook my head, trapped in a situation I didn't want to be in, trying to keep Marlena from causing Chelsea any harm. Hardly able to say the words, I spoke through a clenched jaw. "I'm with Marlena now."

"Oh, honey. I just want you to love and be loved. I want you to be genuinely happy with someone. And I don't care how long it takes. Break it off with Marlena if it's not real love now before it's too late."

"I can't do this." I opened the nearest window and started to crawl through it.

"What the H E double L are you doing, Rex?"

"I'm leaving to find the nearest bar." I slung one leg out. Luckily, the first-floor window ledge was only about 8 feet off the ground.

"What do I tell Marlena?"

"I don't give a—" I sighed "Actually, tell her she might as well get used to this now because this is how it's going to be when she forces me to marry her."

I dropped to the ground and was done for the night.

# FREEDOM TO FLY

## REX

*D*espite the frosty and cold, rainy conditions outside my window, inside this room at the chapel on the country club grounds, the heat was unbearable. I'd already stripped as much of my tux as I possibly could, sweating bullets.

My quiet wedding to Marlena would take place in less than an hour.

I pulled out a flask and gulped down the liquid courage while staring at photos on my phone of the lobby remodel plans, in an attempt to remind myself why I was doing this. But it suddenly meant nothing to me.

I brought up an old photo of Dad and me, in front of a castle in England that our ancestors long ago owned. Sadly, the thought of finally ridding myself of the eyesore the deli was, and all the past trauma that happened there…wasn't so enticing of a reason to tear it down anymore.

The only thing seeing me through this suffering was the photo of Chelsea, dressed as a zombie, accidentally knocking over a lamp.

Why did I care so much about her? She turned down my proposal and hadn't reached out since. Neither had I.

What if I didn't go through with this wedding to Marlena and she goes through with the fake charges against Chelsea? Could I live with that?

So what if Chelsea gets arrested? I could hire her a lawyer and pay her bail and she'd be free in no time, while I'd avoid marrying Marlena altogether.

But the thought of putting Chelsea—such a ray of sunshine —behind bars, arrested for arson, no matter how temporary, didn't sit well with me.

I switched my phone to messages, and scrolled to Chelsea's name, hovering a thumb over the keypad, desperate to send an S.O.S. message, to explain everything, to see what she would have me do. Would she save me?

"Shit." I wouldn't even save me.

At a quarter to my death sentence, the door opened, and I expected it to be Richard, telling me it was time, but to my surprise, Pearl walked in. I scowled.

"What are you doing here?"

"I came to help you escape from this hell you're about to enter. Here. Take my keys and run." She stuffed the keys to her Mercedes SL in my hand. I stared in disbelief.

"Why do you care so much, Pearl? Can't you just leave me alone? There's a reason I'm here today."

"No, I won't let you do this, because I made a promise to your father to look after you two boys. Richard, he was easy to watch over. You, Rex, my God, are such a man-child. But I didn't struggle for years earning my MBA for nothing. It came in handy so I could run this place while you dabbled in whatever suited your fancy."

I scoffed a few feet away. "What do you want from me? To tell you thanks and pat you on the back? Give you a huge raise?"

"I want you to admit you're not happy. Everyone knows it,

and it's high time you face it. You don't like being CEO and you definitely don't want to marry Marlena. And I want you to get your head out of your ass and go after the best thing that ever happened to you—Chelsea."

I had a mind to ream her out for getting into my business, but the door opened again before I could form the words. This time, Mom entered.

"I stopped the wedding," she said.

"You did what?" My hands at my hips, I towered over both ladies.

"I ran into the photographer from the Zombie Ball who spilled the beans about Marlena and her threats to have Chelsea arrested. My boy, I've never known you to make such a sacrifice for someone. I'm so proud of you," Mom said, reaching up and squishing my cheeks between thumb and forefinger. "Obviously, you have a heart and you care for Chelsea."

"What about Marlena?"

"Gone." Mom confirmed. "Once I explained to her father what she was trying to do, well, who cares how he handles it. They are out of our lives. Poof. No more wedding. Merry Christmas,"

I blinked several times, coming to terms with my pardon, my life sentence revoked.

"He's still standing here," Pearl whispered to Mom.

"Perhaps we need a deeper explanation?" She whispered back. "Rex, I offered Pearl the position of interim CEO until the board figures out who will be the next CEO of Buchanan."

"Miriam and I talked about how things have been around the office and the company since you took over, and she was open to the idea," Pearl said.

"Yes, I was. In fact, I'm rather enthused to see what a woman can do with this company for once."

"Why thank you, Miriam. I won't let you down."

"What the fu—" Mom stopped me with her finger. "—am I supposed to do now?"

"Ugh. Rex, don't worry about the company anymore. Worry about *you*. Take some time off and figure yourself out. Get back into real estate. Travel. In fact, I hear Holly Creek is lovely this time of year," Mom said.

"Holly Creek? Why would I want to go—"

"Oh my. He's a little slow sometimes in the romance department, isn't he?" Mom shook her head as an aside to Pearl, who crossed her arms and nodded.

I scoffed at them both. "What do you want me to do, go after Chelsea?"

"Now he's getting it," Pearl said, and Mom nodded.

"She won't want to see me. I broke her heart."

"But you want her, don't you?" Mom shook her head. "And when did a Buchanan ever let anything stop us from getting what we want?"

Slowly it all sunk in. Everything she and Pearl did for me, the opportunity they were giving me to start over. To fly away. I just needed to take the chance and try, no matter if Chelsea would take me back or not. "Actually, Mom, she's not only what I want, she's what I need." I grabbed my jacket and headed for the door.

"Stop, Rex. You can't go empty-handed." Mom hustled up to me, twisting a ring off her finger. "Take this ring. It's the one your father gave to me the night he proposed. It's a simple princess cut emerald ring surrounded by small diamonds. May it bring you luck and love."

I gaped at not only the size and clarity of the gems, but the color, too. The green shining in the light reminded me of Chelsea's eyes.

"It's perfect. Thank you, Mom." I hugged her for the first time in forever, and I grabbed Pearl, too. "I don't know what I would do without you two."

"You're free to fly, now get out of here, and bring Chelsea to dinner soon."

"You're assuming she'll take me back and try again?"

Mom cupped my cheek. "Rex, you have the Buchanan charm and looks and smarts. And now, maybe a little humility. She won't be able to resist you."

I ran out through the empty chapel and parking lot to Pearl's car, grateful I didn't have to face Marlena again.

Once I figured out how to get to Holly Creek, my mind raced there ahead of me in the car. What I would say to Chelsea when I arrived?

"How about I'm a dumbass, for starters?"

I ached to feel my arms around her. To kiss her...to make love with her.

Flooded with thoughts about what was ahead, the worries intensified as nightfall and snow started falling. The roads turned slick and I hoped to hell the Mercedes would get me back to her arms safely.

# HOLLY CREEK OR BUST

## CHELSEA

"I'm stuffed. I'll need to switch to sweatpants if you keep feeding us this way, Mom." Maisy unbuttoned the top button of her jeans after the Christmas Eve meal.

"If you ask me, you were too skinny to begin with." Mom patted her cheek as she collected empty plates from the table.

"Come on. We'll turn on the radio and dance in the kitchen to burn calories while helping Mom clean up." I practically dragged her with me.

"I'll come help, too," Aunt Louisa said.

"I'll stay here and keep watch on Uncle Doug," Colt chortled, knowing he got the easy job. He grabbed a card deck out of the sideboard. "How about a game of Gin Rummy, Uncle?"

"You know me. I never turn down a game of cards."

In the kitchen, there we were, four fine women dancing away to golden oldies from the fifties, washing, scrubbing, rinsing, drying, and the chore was done before we knew it.

"Just in time. We have the Holly Creek community caroling tonight," Mom reminded us. "I'll put the kettle on and make thermoses of hot cocoa. You girls dig out all the mittens, hats, scarves, boots, and jackets. The storm that passed through here yesterday covered the ground, and even though the snow plows cleared the streets, it'll be slick. Grab the flashlights, too."

"We know." Maisy and I replied in unison. The holiday experience in Holly Creek hadn't changed as long as I could remember. Christmas Eve always involved the town caroling. We'd walk the Main Street and route through some of the side streets singing traditional Christmas music, ending up at the community center for pies baked by Mom and Flora's Diner. It was BYOC—Bring Your Own Cocoa.

I couldn't wait. I joined Maisy in digging through the closet by the front door, only to find her sitting on the floor trying to match mittens with her phone in her hands.

"Texting Brooks?" I worked faster at matching things up.

"Yes. He's so sweet. Look at the photo he sent. He opened my gift early and is wearing the scarf I knitted him."

She showed the photo of him with a broad grin, proudly wearing the scarf of variegated blue colors. Maisy was determined to get the hang of knitting, and that one was her third attempt, much better than the first two.

"He's so dang cute." Her smile right now... I knew that look, the look of infatuation or lust or love, when just thinking about the special man in your life can put the glow of longing into your eyes and smile. Sometimes I recognized that look in myself when good memories of Rex came back to me...but then remembering that night at the rooftop and the glow faded.

"You really like him, don't you?" I asked.

Her cheeks pinked, and she put the phone away, sighing and reaching for the scarves next. "Yeah. But I made the decision to apply for the Scientific Fleet of Oceanic Enterprises. If I get accepted to the research team, I'll spend all summer and fall traveling and working, only back in time for Christmas next year. Brooks has been hinting lately about taking a vacation together after I graduate and making all kinds of plans for us after that. I don't know how to tell him I might not be here."

I covered her hand with mine. I used to think she should focus on work and forget about distractions from men, but now? All I just wanted for her was to live life and be happy. "Take it slow and easy, Maisy. I have a feeling Brooks really likes you, too, and will stick around for a while. Maybe he'd wait for you and pick up where you left off when you return?"

A knock on the door above our heads scared the heck out of us. "Who the heck could that be on Christmas Eve?" I exclaimed.

The knocking turned to pounding. "Chelsea? Chelsea? Please be in there."

That sounded like Rex. Couldn't be. "Hurry, Maisy." We shoved all the winter clothes and boots back into the closet and scrambled up. My breath caught at the sight of Rex's face in the door's window.

I flung the door open, focused on his face, like I forgot what he looked like. "Rex? What are you doing here? You can't just show up and crash another family's Christmas Eve."

"Why not? What if you're the woman for me and this is the family I should have been with all along?"

My heart jumped. "Don't do that. Play all the What Ifs."

"Okay, fine. Then how about this story? I'm a dumbass and there's a woman I've never been able to forget. So in an effort to spend what remains of the holidays with her, I drove to a small town, only to hit a snowstorm, crash my car, freeze for hours, finally walk across ice and snow until a truck picked me up. Then, was dropped in Holly Creek where everything was closed and I had to find people to tell me where she lives. Does that suit your sensibility better?" He coughed into his sleeve.

"You really did all that?"

"What does it look like? Yes, Chelsea. I crashed a Mercedes SL. Ruined a damn good pair of leather shoes, and this tuxedo is beyond repair now and definitely not enough to keep the chill off. I don't even have my b-bag to change clothes because the car went over a little c-c-cliff." He coughed more, almost hoarse by the end of his tirade.

"Chelsea, let the man inside. It's cold out there," Mom admonished, coming up behind me to see what was the commotion.

I snapped out of it and pulled him in. Maisy shut the door behind him. Rex coughed more, but from his intense body heat radiating to me, I knew instantly something was wrong. I put the back of my hand to his forehead.

"Oh no. You have a fever. Mom!" I cried.

"I'll get my medical kit. You get him to the bathroom for a quick bathing. Colt, get some clothes for him to change into. Maisy, heat up some chicken broth," she barked orders, and everyone jumped into action.

"I'm fine. Just give me a c-cup of c-c-coffee." He started shivering as I ducked under his arm and helped him down the hall to the bathroom. "I h-had to s-s-see you, Ch-Ch—"

"Sh. Rex, you're here, but you're feverish. I'll take care of you for now. There'll be plenty of time for talking later."

In the bathroom, I finally got over my initial shock and took in his pale appearance and condition. He'd braved a storm to get to me. But what did this mean? Was he here to make another pitch to marry for all the wrong reasons?

A COUPLE HOURS LATER, in my room, Rex slept while I kept a constant vigil in a chair next to my bed, changing the cold washcloth on his head often. Everyone else went out to the festivities in town, leaving us alone in the house. I didn't mind missing it; I was only worried about him and what he was doing here.

I reached up and fingered the hair on his forehead. The typically virile man slept like a baby after taking medicine and drinking a little broth. The fever weakened him, hopefully only temporarily.

I hadn't talked to him or seen him for almost two months, but certainly thought and wondered about him. If I was honest, I even fantasized that somehow we might find our way back together and try again one day, under different circumstances.

Never did I think he'd show up on my doorstep on Christmas Eve. I still couldn't believe he was in Holly Creek. Had he changed, or was he desperate and still after the same things he wanted, my hand in marriage for his precious building remodel?

He stirred, and I stood, leaning over him and feeling his chest a little clammy. I untucked the sheet a little, when I felt a hand on my thigh. I gasped and locked eyes with him.

"Hi, sweetness." He half spoke, half coughed.

"Hi. Don't talk. Try to rest."

"That's hard to do when I have so much to say to you."

"I know." A stray tear rolled down my cheek for some reason, and he caught it.

"Don't cry." Somehow his touch on my cheek and nearly hoarse voice were even sexier and set my heart racing. Why couldn't I resist Rex Buchanan?

"I'll be fine. I just need you to rest so you can get better fast. Then we'll talk and figure all this out between us."

"Promise you won't run away?" His face took on a boyish quality, and I just wanted to eat him right up. But I had to remember our last conversation on the rooftop. Clearly, our goals didn't align. He wanted me to marry just to get what he wanted. Not for love. But talking would help bring closure.

"Yes, promise. I'm not going anywhere. The deli's closed for the holidays. I don't report back to the TV station until the second week of January. Besides, the roads aren't the best to drive on right now, as you know. Do you have to be anywhere soon?"

"Mom fired me from CEO of the family company. I'm free to do what I want to, and right now, without a car, I'm not going any—" He coughed more. I blinked at the news.

"Sh. We have time then. You rest and get better."

"No, sweetness, I need to talk with you."

"We'll talk when you're better. If you don't mind staying here in Holly Creek and rest for a few days, that is."

"Is that all we'll do is rest and talk?" He tried to be sly about his question, but ended up in a coughing fit that lasted a couple minutes this time. I shook my head and helped him with a glass of water.

Once he quieted down, I forbade him to open his mouth, instead I became chatty, telling him about Holly Creek and all the festivities this week before New Year's Day. "Flora's Diner, my mom's place, is featuring her famous Pie Duo Plate—any two homemade slices with ice cream, and you can pick from pumpkin, apple, cherry, mincemeat. My cousins give horse and sleigh rides through the fields for a few dollars. Some of my friends have businesses in town, so I'll be visiting them and shopping. And the pond is popular for ice skating. Do you know how to ice skate?"

He nodded. Then he scooted over to the other side of the bed and patted the mattress.

"What? You want me to lay there?"

His smile and vigorous head bobbing had me giggling. He was too darn cute right now as my patient. Although he still looked tired, his blue eyes brightened, luring me in. "I don't think that's a good idea, Rex."

"It's the best idea, because I miss you, sweetness. Besides, I'm cold and the best thing to warm up a body is another warm body. You want to nurse me back to good health, don't you?"

I caved in and got under the covers with him, spooning my back into his chest out of habit. "I'm not sure this is proper nursing technique," I teased. He responded with a growl and tightened his hold on me.

"Does that mean don't move?" I asked.

"Yes," he whispered. "Stay with me." His breath feathered across my ear and his chin scruff tickled my neck.

I missed him, his rich scent, his body, and our nights together—and apparently he did too, since something was knocking at my back.

"No, Rex. You need to save your energy."

He growled again, caressing a hand down my body.

"If you won't behave, I'll get out of this bed."

His hand snapped back up into place, and he tightened me to him.

After a minute, I sighed and whispered, "I've missed you, too. But you were such an asshole."

"I know," came his reply.

It didn't take long before I heard his heavy breathing, showing he'd drifted off to sleep. It took me a little while longer, though. A vision came to me, where I was walking in a field of snow at Christmas time wearing a bridal gown.

What did it mean? What did he want? What did *I* want?

Would he be the same old Rex, trying to get me into his scheme for marriage just so he could remodel his precious building? Or did he have a change of heart?

The picture of a white wedding dress in the snow kept nagging me as I tossed and turned beside him all night. Was it a sign? Could Rex and I find some way to make this work? Could this be my last Christmas as a Miss?

# THE BEST PRESENT

## REX

"*I* can think of much better ways to use my tongue." I winked at Chelsea, standing next to her in front of the dresser in her room. Clearly, feeling much better, I believed my fever broke, but she had to be sure.

"Stop. This is serious. You landed on our doorstep with a fever last night. Now put this under your tongue, hold it there, and quit talking." She stuffed the glass thermometer just so in my mouth, unusually grumpy for my typically sunshiny lady.

I took it out again and tried hard to make her laugh. "You're really turning me on, taking care of me like this. Remind me to buy you a nurse costume. I can see this fantasy playing out really nicely for me." I popped the stick back under my tongue and wiggled my brows. Her head cocked at me with crossed arms told me to be serious.

"You're making some big assumptions there, considering we haven't talked yet."

I was. Hell was waking up next to Chelsea on Christmas morning hard as a rock and not being able to do anything about it, since she insisted we talk, and that I shouldn't exert myself until my fever was gone. I willed the mercury to stay in the normal range, while my stiff cock twitched, dying to be inside of her again.

It was early morning on Christmas, and no one else in the house stirred but us. Waiting the few minutes for the thermometer to register and not being able to talk to Chelsea or touch her was extremely painful.

When time was up, she removed the implement from my mouth, inspecting it with laser concentration. "Wow, Mr. Buchanan. Looks like you've made a miraculous recovery overnight. You're back to normal temperature. But you do still have a cough, so take it easy today. Don't overly exert yourself with strenuous activities."

"Yes, Nurse Chelsea." I grabbed her and dipped her, eager to taste her again. "Does this count as strenuous?" I nuzzled into her cleavage, kissing and drawing my lips across her skin.

"Oh. That-that should be fine," she sighed as if I took her breath away.

I brought her upright, continuing to pursue with kisses from her neck to her earlobe, delighting in her breathing turning into tiny moans. "And this—too much?" I kissed the sensitive spot I knew well under her ear.

"Stop, Rex. We need to talk. Your kisses are confusing the situation." She broke out of my reach.

"I disagree. My thoughts and intentions are clear as day, after I spent the better part of the past two months living under a dark cloud of shame and guilt. Fuck, Chelsea, if I could take back that night on the rooftop, I would. Who the hell did I think I was then? Yes, I've always been a bit of a spoiled billionaire, but your face when you gave back the ring broke me. Killed me. Stabbed me in the heart." I jabbed my chest for extra measure.

"Good, because you hurt me so much that night." She brushed a tear away.

"Baby..." I stepped up to her and cupped her cheeks, re-familiarizing myself with the depths of her green irises. "I can't stand the thought of how badly I hurt you, but I think that night was necessary to wake me up to the man I'm supposed to be. *With you.*"

She sputtered, more tears forming at the corners of her eyes. "Your words sound good, and I want to trust them."

"You can. But if I need to prove myself to you again, every single day I will. Tell me what I need to do. I'm not in charge of Buchanan Energy now. I'm so far removed from the building, I don't care about it anymore. My stress level has returned to normal. I can go back to doing what I love with my real estate investments. You'll find I'm a different man, but with the same heart that beats *only* for you." My lips claimed hers with gentle persuasion. But only one lingering kiss. I couldn't be bullish about this. I needed patience to bring her back around to me.

"Rex, I missed you, but I don't know. I can't stop thinking about you and wondering what might have happened if things were different, if we were different. But we can't go backwards."

"We are different now, sweetness; *I'm* different now. I believe everything that happened changed me for the better. Please, give us a chance to try again." I fingered her locks, but a tickle in my throat caused me to cough again.

"We shouldn't be talking so much, aggravating your cough. Come on, back to bed." She sat on the edge and patted it. "I'm wondering if we should take you to the urgent care today?"

"I'm fine. I weathered the storm to get back to you. You're all the medicine I need." I got back in bed and pulled her to me before she escaped. We settled in, but she was quiet and I could feel her shutting down. I couldn't rest, needing to keep going, to explain, to plead, to grovel, whatever it took to get her back.

I lifted on my elbow to see her face. "So much has happened. Things I need for you know." I broke down and told her about Marlena and my personal hell of the past two months.

Her brow creased as if angry. "I wish you would have

reached out and told me what was going on. We could have battled her together, gone to the police, tried to explain."

"It's done now. I'd do it all again, put myself through hell, if it meant protecting you. Thankfully, Mom came to my rescue, and I didn't have to go through with marrying her. What about you and the show? Do you enjoy working there?"

"Stanley told me you're the one who recommended me."

"Ah, I told him not to."

"I guess I should thank you for the opportunity."

"Hey, no, all I did was put your name in front of him and show him your social media posts. *You* did the rest, charming him and everyone who watches that show with your sunshine. You're so good at it. I can't tear my eyes away—"

"You watch?"

I brushed the back of my hand on her cheek. "Every single episode, a dozen times each, and I think I can recite your recipes from memory now."

She relaxed into a chuckle and shared with me all about her TV work and her plans for the deli, her eyes lighting up with the passion she had for it all.

"For the record, I need for you to know that my old feelings about the deli are gone. The building means nothing to me and I threw away plans to remodel. Instead of the past when I think about that place, I see you, sweetness, all your sunshiny ways, making people happy with your food, and killing them with kindness." I chuckled, and she joined me. "You cured me. You're all I want."

"I'm busier than ever, now, though, Rex."

I squeezed her to me. "Maybe you won't have time for me anymore, then."

She peered up at me. "I used to think, in order to achieve my goals and work hard, I couldn't make room for a man or love. But now...I realize it's all about balancing the areas of my life in order to be totally fulfilled."

"Love...?" I ran my fingers through her hair and down her jaw, lifting her chin so our eyes locked so she'd know I was serious. "I do love you, Chelsea. Why do you think I risked so much coming to Holly Creek? The entire journey here, I had no idea what you'd do when I found you. You could have slammed the door in my face and left me out to freeze to death and I would have gladly died of a broken heart if you had, because at least I tried to get to you and make one last appeal for you to take me back. I'm a broken man who loves you."

"There's always been something between us too strong to understand. I thought we were over, that there was no way you could redeem yourself after that night on the roof, but you happened upon my doorstep on Christmas Eve, of all days." A shadow of worry and doubt crossed her eyes still. "I want so badly for you to be the best present I've ever had."

"No, *you're* the best *I've* ever had. I love you, Chelsea. Please forgive me. I'll do whatever it takes to be the man you need. Fuck, you have no idea how much I want to buy your love, to offer you the world, my money, my possessions if you'd just take me back. But now I know there's only one thing I can give you that'll mean the most to you. My heart. And you have it; it's yours, but will you take it? Take me back? Give me another chance?"

I sweated what seemed an eternity for her reply as she searched my eyes. My heart ached for her as if she reached in and twisted it just to see how strong I was in my resolve to be better for her.

## 28

# BELIEVE AGAIN

## REX

*T*he tension between us weighed heavily in the small bed of Chelsea's room. Finally, after waiting next to her for what felt like an eternity, a warm curve of lips appeared across her face. "I love you, too, Rex," she whispered.

"Oh, sweetness. We can try again? I know we'll get it right this time."

"Yes. Again. But don't break my heart a second time," she warned.

A sigh of relief left me, and I gathered her in my arms. "I won't. Thank you, baby. Christmas used to be my *least* favorite holiday after Dad passed away. Now, it'll always be the day I found my way back to you."

We held each other close, my heart surging with hope again. I vowed to spend each day proving my love for her.

"Merry Christmas, Rex." She kissed my chest. "I'm sorry I don't have a present for you, but there might be something we could give each other." Her hand reached down between us and under my sweats, wrapping her fingers around my cock, hard as a rock and more than ready to give.

"I have a huge package for you, and feels like you found it."

Her laughter broke any remaining tension in the room.

I reclaimed her lips as mine, and would not waste another minute apart. I covered her body, nesting between her legs, pressing my heat into her core. But it wasn't enough. I need us both bare, skin to skin, hearts and souls burning together. I lifted and removed Colt's Prima the Diva of Rock t-shirt while Chelsea unbuttoned her flannel nightgown. Then I lost patience and yanked both sides; the buttons flew off everywhere.

"Rex! That was my favorite nighty."

"I said I wouldn't buy your love, but I'll buy you ten more of those." I stopped and gaped at her creamy skin, the fullness of her breasts, and most of all, the lack of panties covering her mound. "Were you naked under the nightgown all night?"

She sheepishly shrugged. "Maybe. I wanted you, but I also wanted to be sure we talked and worked things out."

"Have you gotten everything you wanted?" I'd give her the world if she wanted it. I needed her that much. "Have we done enough talking for now?"

"Yes. All done talking."

I hovered over her, one elbow by her shoulder, my hand trailing up her thigh, to her stomach, and palming her breast. Her arms circled my neck, threading fingertips through my hair.

"Does Nurse Chelsea clear me for activity?" My fingers retreated down to the apex of her thighs, finding her hot and ready for me. I teased a finger along her wet seam.

"Oh, yes, Mr. Buchanan. Make your move." She lifted, sucking on my bottom lip and moaning. I snaked a finger through her folds, finding her hard nub, but I became impatient to connect with her.

"I need inside of you, and I don't want a fucking condom to come between us."

"I'm still on the pill. But did...did you and that Marlena ever...?" Fear flashed through her eyes.

"Fuck no. Strike that thought from your head right now. Baby, I pined away for you so hard. But...what about you?" It hadn't occurred to me before that she could have been dating others for the past few months.

"There's only been you since the first night we were together in the Hamptons on your boat."

"Then I'm taking you, and claiming you, making you mine. No other man will touch you ever again, hear me?"

"Yes, Rex. Take me."

I shoved my sweats down and notched at her seam, taking a delicious minute to slide in, locking eyes with her the entire way. Inch by inch, her walls stretched to mold to me and I lost all sense of time and space, losing myself to her completely.

Only when I was balls deep, knocking on her soul, did I crash upon her lips. She reached her hands down to my buttocks, writhing, urging me to move.

I began my charge, in what would be my greatest victory, capturing her body, heart, and soul, and if I had my way, it'd be forever. I held those thoughts close to my heart for our future. For now, we found a perfect rhythm.

"Oh sweetness, you rock my soul." This wasn't just any fuck; we made love. Our hands laced together above her head. Her body beneath mine moved like an extension of myself. We were one.

"Yes, harder, Rex." We gained steam, taking and giving, gasping for air. Cheek to cheek, I thrust into her, deepening my strokes. Never had I submitted my entire self to a woman so passionately. The experience shook me to my core, and I was losing it.

"I love you, Chelsea. I can't hold back much longer." A cough caught in my throat.

"I love you, too. Shift onto your back. I'll take it from here."

We turned together, locked in limbs, never losing contact.

She took over, riding me, playing with her clit. Her moans intensified. "I'm close."

"That's it, baby. Come on my cock." I planted my feet and matched her movements, thrusting my hips. Her walls tightened, her legs shook, and I marveled at the contortions on her face as she came undone, moaning my name over and over.

"I'm there with you, Chelsea, milk me dry." Everything I had spilled into her, burying deep, her walls squeezing every drop out of me. She collapsed on top of me and I held onto her until our heartbeats calmed to a natural pace.

"How soon can we make love again?" She chuckled. I started to, as well, but coughed.

"My recovery time might need to be a little longer right now." I couldn't wait for the next round.

"That's fine. We have nothing but time together on this Christmas break. And I already know who I'll be kissing on New Year's Eve night. *You.* If you'll stay here all week." She shifted beside me, laying her head on my chest. "I think you'll find the Holly Creek community's First Night party is a real blast."

"I have no car, no way to leave, and I wouldn't want to. Not now, not when we've just started again." I didn't think I'd leave her side anytime soon for fear of her slipping away.

"The storm was nasty. I'm so thankful you made it through. What if something had happened to you and you didn't make it here?"

"Sh. We're not doing the what-ifs, remember?" I hated her worrying, although in hindsight, she's right. I was much too anxious to reach her when I left New York City to check the weather or to fear for my safety. "Tell me who to call and I'll see if I can get the car towed and fixed."

"This is Holly Creek, and with so much snow dumped on us and being Christmas, the roads won't clear for a few days, or the mechanic might have taken the week off. Guess we're rather far removed from civilization and sunshine for your tastes," she teased.

"You're wrong. I have all the sunshine I need right here in my arms."

"Aw, Rex. I can't believe I'm in Holly Creek with you. I never thought it possible to get you out of New York City, much less that we'd be back together."

"Hey, I leave the city once in a while. I take my boat out every summer and cruise the islands."

"Don't tell Maisy that. She'll hound you for every detail. While I love snow, she's a beach person. We've already blocked out the week of her spring break to go somewhere fun."

"Send me the dates. We'll take the yacht and sail to any island you want."

"Really? You would do that with us? I'd love that."

"And I'd love to see you wearing nothing but bikinis in the sunshine, lounging on my boat."

She chortled. "Of course you would."

"So what exactly is there to do around here, anyway? I mean, I plan to spend a good chunk of time with you in bed, but at some point, we need to eat and find some entertainment. Are there any five-star restaurants in Holly Creek? Plays to see?"

"Listen, city boy, we have plenty of wonderful things for you to see and do in Holly Creek. I dare you to fall in love with this place."

"I'm already in love with *you*."

She pecked at my lips. "I don't think I'd tire of hearing you say that."

"Because of you, and your love for this place, I'm sure I'll give Holly Creek a fair try."

"It's the most magical time of year to be here, well, except for Christmas in July, of course." Her lips curved, forming a warm smile, and filled my heart with hope that we'd have many more Christmases together. "Actually, I'll be right back."

She got up and dug through the drawer, finding another flannel nighty to put on. I'd rip the buttons off on that one, as well. Nothing would be a barrier between us anymore.

I heard her in the bathroom down the hall cleaning up, and when she returned, she kneeled next to me on the mattress, unfolding a paper in her hand.

"What's that?"

"When you told me some time ago that Christmas wasn't your favorite holiday, I decided I would try to change your mind. So, I wrote out Rex's Bucket List for Christmas."

I howled. My girl was too much. "Okay, tell me the first thing on the list."

"Ice skating...although at the time I wrote this, we were in New York City, so it says at Rockefeller Plaza. But now, in Holly Creek, that'd be at the pond where all the locals go to skate, play pickup games of hockey, and drink hot cocoa."

"Perfect. Here's the plan. We'll make love again, then get up and shower together, enjoy Christmas with your family. I can't wait to meet your mom and brother, by the way. And finally, ice skate this afternoon. And every day until New Year's Eve, I want to tackle that list with you."

We held each other and talked more about our plans for the week. Whatever she wanted, I'd do, because somehow it happened. I fell deeply, madly in love with a woman who had the brightest soul.

"Thank you, sweetness, for taking me back, and for loving me despite my faults. You've turned this Christmas into the best ever. I don't see how anything could ever top this," I said.

"You never know what the future holds for us. But as long as we face it together, anything is possible." She winked a gleaming green eye at me, and I hugged her closer.

I used to believe I was a lucky man, with all my family's wealth and possessions. But now, my life was richer, with Chelsea in it.

# 29

# IT HAPPENED ON VALENTINE'S

## THE REAL PROPOSAL

### CHELSEA CALHOUN

"*S*top fussing." Rex playfully slapped my hand away from putting more finishing touches to the posters. "Everything looks great."

"I just want to send Colt off to the Navy with all the love we can show him." He and Mom drove down to New York City, and later today, we'd drop him at the bus depot to report for duty. The bus would drive him to Great Lakes for boot camp. But first, the family was having brunch together some place fancy, and Rex insisted on treating us all.

"I know you're worried about him, just like you always worry for Maisy. That's what makes me think you'll be an excellent mother. Someday." He emphasized the last word, standing beside me and rubbing my back.

I stared at him, sort of shocked. We hadn't talked about kids yet, not seriously. "Mother? Well, you know what else kids need? A good father."

"According to Miriam, she seems to think I'd make a good

father. Someday," he winked, again with extra emphases on the last word.

I admired my handsome man, always surprising me around every turn. The alarm on my phone went off. "That's my alarm to jump in to the shower and get ready for the brunch. But do you really think the posters are finished?" I dabbed my paint brush a little more here and there.

"Are you kidding? Yes. They are. And look, you just moved in with me and now you've got paint and glitter everywhere." He eyed my project like a billionaire who doesn't like a mess in his pristine home.

"Get used to it, buddy. You asked me to live with you, and I'm not as much of a neat freak as you are. Plus, didn't you just mention being parents a minute ago? You realize kids can be very messy?" I bumped my ass against him.

"Oh, don't even bump me with that fine ass or I'll spank you for this mess, and whatever else I want to do to you."

"Rex! Didn't you get enough of me last night?"

"Never." He kissed my forehead.

The insatiable appetite of this man…but I wasn't complaining. Since Christmas, we'd been inseparable and things were going so well between us. This time around was night and day compared to before the *rooftop disaster*, as I referred to it.

We still had incredible chemistry and connection, like always, but our time in Holly Creek over Christmas and New Year's did us a lot of good. We talked about everything, and discussed our goals and realized we align in so many ways. He's a different Rex now, focused on his real estate business, and not having to worry about the family company now that it was in Pearl's very capable hands.

I had good employees managing the deli now, so I could focus on my work full-time at the TV station. And, just like Stanley predicted, I'd been approached by a major publisher to write a recipe book featuring many of the comfort foods from my Morning City Show segments.

To top it all off, last week, Rex insisted I move in with him. But I had a little hesitation about how fast things were moving between us. We met in September, broke up early November, reunited on Christmas day, and now it was Valentine's. After we talked it out, he helped me realize that there's no right or wrong here, no manual to follow for how slow or fast a relationship should go.

We just needed to do what we felt was best for us. So I moved in, and, honestly, the timing felt absolutely right. Every day with him got better than the last.

"Oh look, this one doesn't have glitter on the C of Colt's name." I reached for the glue and red, white, and blue glitter, but Rex put his arms around my waist.

"Back away from the glitter and paint. I think you got enough on you now." He howled. "You're a mess."

He picked me up by the waist and carried me all the way to the bathroom. "I'm going to dump you under the shower head."

"No," I giggled. "Don't you dare. Put me down. Enough!" I warned him.

He stopped in front of the shower, holding me in his arms while slowly reaching for the handle to turn on the water.

"Rex, I mean it."

"How about a deal? We'll shower together. I'll soap you up and check you for glitter everywhere…in every crevice."

I caved in too easily because I couldn't resist Rex Buchanan, my billionaire.

After undressing, we held each other under the water at first and he caressed my back. My heart had become so full from his love.

"I hope this time we'll last and continue to grow together." Turning my face up to him, I added the three words that came to mean so much between us. "I love you."

"We will." He melted his lips on mine. "And I love you, Chelsea."

### Rex Buchanan

As far as Chelsea knew, this brunch was in celebration of Colt heading off to boot camp. There was another reason entirely, and I had everyone in on it but her.

Since we got back together, surprising Chelsea became my favorite hobby. I was always leaving notes lying around in unexpected places for her to find. Bought tickets for us to attend concerts or plays together. I even jetted us off to a spa getaway one weekend.

I loved spending money on her, mostly because she didn't take me or money for granted, often sometimes chastising me for spending too much on her. But it would never be enough. I'd spoil her, but I could never picture her turning spoiled or bratty.

Today would be my biggest surprise yet. We were to meet our families at Tetto, an Italian five-star restaurant in one of the high-rise buildings I own with incredible views of Manhattan. But I purposely made us late, hence our shower together after painting the posters for Colt.

When we arrived at Tetto, every table was empty, just like I'd requested, since I reserved the entire venue for the day.

"Oh no. Are you sure they're open?" Chelsea asked given how quiet it was as we stepped off the elevator, except for some kitchen noise.

"Supposed to be." I scratched the back of my head and really played it up. "I think I hear some sound over there. Let's walk to the other end and see if maybe brunch is served down there."

I had her walk in front of me, mostly so I could admire the

way her tan suede thigh-high boots made her ass shimmy in a body-hugging cream-colored sweater dress. Buying her clothes was another new hobby of mine, and I'd picked this outfit for her, especially for this occasion.

The sound got louder as we reached a door on the opposite end of the restaurant, but we soon realized it was music. "I think we're supposed to go in here."

I opened the door and watched her face as she entered to the scene before her. Her eyes darted around and her face contorted. "Rex, what did you do?"

I took her by the hand and led her down a white aisle runner sprinkled with red rose petals, to a seven foot tall heart, covered completely in red roses—Except for two words spelled out in white roses across the middle: Marry Me.

Music softly played for us by a string quartet off to the side, and the walls of the room were decorated floor to ceiling with white linen curtains. The potent scent of roses wafted through the room and everything was just as I wanted it for her.

I got down on bended knee to deliver the most important speech of my life.

I took her hand, and a deep breath, and noticed she was already crying before I'd even begun.

"Boy, I really fucked this up last time. Didn't I?"

She laughed so hard she snorted, bringing her hand to her nose. "Yes, you did."

"So I'm pretty sure whatever I do this time is going to top that. But you know what? I just wanted to keep it simple. Last time I had all these plans and elaborate schemes and promises of money and buying you things, all to convince you to marry me and give me what I want. What a mess that was, right?"

"Yes." She reached her hand out and fingered my hair off my forehead. I was kind of sweating it, even though I had confidence in what her answer would be.

"This time, there's only one thing I'm offering. My heart."

"Oh, Rex."

"And this time, there's only one thing I want. Your heart."

She cried, and could no longer move her hands fast enough to stop the tears from rolling down. I reached a hand up to help.

"I know, it's been sort of a whirlwind relationship, so fast, bumpy yet easy at the same time. Everything between us feels right. It did from the beginning, but we just didn't have our acts together. Well, I didn't. Thankfully, you gave me a second chance and now? Everyday with you is one I don't take for granted."

One of the violinists broke away and brought Chelsea a handful of tissues and we laughed and thanked them.

"So I don't see why I should have to wait another year before I ask to spend the rest of our lives together when I already know that's what I want to do. Chelsea Ruth Calhoun, would you do me the absolute honor of marrying me and being my wife?"

I held out the emerald ring Mom had given me. My parents had a pretty good marriage filled with love for each other, so hopefully this ring brought good luck. I pushed it onto her ring finger, and it fit perfectly.

"It's so beautiful! Yes, Rex, I'll marry you."

I stood, and she launched into my arms, and I swung her around. "Thank you, sweetness. You've made me the happiest I've ever been."

After a few more kisses, I called out. "Okay everyone, you can come in now."

Through the curtains, our families emerged upon us, hugging and congratulating.

My mother, who adored Chelsea, was the first to come up to us. "Oh, Rex, that was so beautiful." What a touching moment of Mom gazing upon me lovingly. But it only lasted a second. "Now, Chelsea, next week, I have an appointment set up for lunch with the city's top wedding planner. The ceremony will be at the Fifth Avenue Church, of course. And I've already checked on dates at the Plaza Hotel for the reception. How do you feel about a Christmas wedding? I know it only gives us about ten months to plan but—"

"Mom," I warned. Chelsea had the deer in the headlights look, so I interrupted. "Do you think you can let my future bride and I just enjoy the day today? Save the planning fest for next week."

"Oh, you're right. I'm just so excited. We're finally going to have a Buchanan wedding. And it's going to be perfect, mark my words." Miriam hugged us and moved on to talk to the rest of the family.

"Um. What did you just get me into?" Chelsea buried her face in my lapel.

"Don't worry, sweetness. We'll get through this together. You'll see. I love you, you love me, and that's all that'll ever matter."

THE END...FOR now.

# IT HAPPENED SERIES

## STEAMY SMALL TOWN BILLIONAIRE ROMANCES

**What to read next:** Enjoy more stories in the series with Richard, Brooks, Archer and more characters you'll love in **the It Happened Series:**

### It Happened Series, Available in KU:

Book 1: It Happened—Rex and Chelsea (this one)

Book 2: It Happened in Paris—Richard and Vivian

Book 3: It Happened Again—Brooks and Maisy

Book 4: It Happened in Vegas—Keaton and Sophie

Book 5: It Happened After Hours—Griffon and Jessa (coming August 2025)

Book 6: It Happened to Us—Archer and Penny (coming October 2025)

If you enjoyed this book, kindly leave a review. Thank you!

Xoxo Zee

# EPILOGUE

## IT HAPPENED ONE CHRISTMAS WEDDING

### Chelsea

To most brides, this might be their dream—a blank check. I stared down at it in my hands, signed and written on the account of Miriam Buchanan-Astor.

"Whatever it takes, no matter the cost, we'll plan the fanciest wedding New York City has *ever* seen," Miriam said, and took a delicate bite of a petite cucumber sandwich. As far as future mother-in-laws were concerned, I imagined there might be worse.

I gaped up at Rex, my gorgeous groom, who grinned and nodded to the check, his eyebrow arching toward his fabulous head of dark hair. "And whatever Mom doesn't cover, I will. You have carte blanche, Chelsea. Anything you want, it's yours for our wedding day."

I glanced around the afternoon champagne tea at the Palm Court restaurant in the Plaza Hotel, where people dressed in fancy clothes enjoyed tea, tiny sandwiches, and scones on fine china. The soaring stained-glass dome overhead, a signature historical architectural feature here, let in bright light for such a late February day, making the emerald and diamonds in my engagement ring shine that much more.

It all seemed a bit surreal. Could this really be my life right now? A year ago, I was in Holly Creek managing Flora's Diner for my mother. My life took an enormous turn in September when I moved to New York City, took over Uncle Doug's deli, and met Rex.

"I don't honestly know what to say. And I can't imagine the wedding I'm thinking about costing much. My mother bakes the best pies, and we can fill a table with them at the reception. And there's a quaint gazebo in Holly Creek I always imagined getting married at, but maybe we could find one here—"

"Chelsea, dear…" Miriam cut me off, placating me with a pat on my hand. "Perhaps you need to think *bigger*. I'm expecting at least three hundred guests. How many should we expect from your side?" She asked with a raised manicured eyebrow.

The number struck me hard, and for a moment, I sat there dumbfounded, taking in Miriam's exquisitely fashioned appearance for a mature woman. Then again, money probably made that easier for her. I'd yet to see her undone, with no makeup, dyed hair brushed out, or even with a pair of yoga pants on her thin hips. Was there ever a time she just let herself go?

"Oh, let's see. There's simply my close family of 4, a handful of friends, a few work associates. Some cousins. Plus ones, um, maybe twenty?" I provided.

"Well," a polite, polished, all-knowing grin spread across her face. "You see, there's a Buchanan tradition to uphold. They have held all weddings at Fifth Avenue Church, as yours will be. And your reception will be here, at the Plaza's Grand Ballroom. I've already secured the room."

"Here?" I studied Rex, questioning him silently. He sheepishly looked away.

"Yes. You cannot possibly expect all my guests to travel to

Holly Creek for the wedding, right?" She blinked innocently at me but with a hint of manipulation, as if she'd thought about this conversation well in advance and played me like a fiddle.

I was certain I was only imagining it though, as I knew her only concern here was making sure this wedding didn't cancel, compared to her eldest son's wedding a few years prior, an event that displeased her and embarrassed her among her high society friends.

"Of course, we'll take care of all the accommodations for your family and guests to come to New York City for the wedding. We'll put them up here at the Plaza Hotel." Rex was quick to add.

"Okay, that's kind of you." A trip to the city for the holidays was always a nice idea and something my family and friends would likely enjoy. But money was a touchy subject sometimes with people from different backgrounds. I didn't come from much, and I often floundered, bewildered at the enormity of the money Rex's family possessed.

"The Plaza will be beautiful for our wedding, won't it?" Miriam didn't necessarily ask, more like stating.

"It's just a lot to take in." I worried at Miriam's use of the word *our*.

"I know, Chelsea, dear, which is why I hired Agnes Hightower, one of New York's finest wedding planners." She finished her glass of champagne. "She'll work with us in putting all of this together."

"Oh, yes. That'll be very helpful." The tension in my shoulders let up a little.

"Oh, there's Pierre, the general manager of the Plaza, waiting to give us a tour of the ballroom. So finish up your tea and I'll meet you right over there."

Miriam left our table, and I waited to speak until she was out of earshot, walking toward a tall man in a dark suit, who I assumed was Pierre.

Then I turned to Rex. "I've never been given a blank check for anything. It scares me. It's too much to handle."

"I can't tell you how much I love hearing you say that. It's why I'm positive you can manage this. You're not going to be out there spending on every frivolous thing—not that I mind if you do, because whatever you want, you get. Especially if you spend some of that frivolity on sexy lingerie for our wedding night and our honeymoon." He smoldered his heated gaze at me.

"That could be arranged." I teased back, rubbing his thigh under the table, but I quickly reverted to my worries. "I just want our day to be special, Rex."

"It will be, Sweetness, and trust me, you're going to love it here at the Plaza. Besides, despite all this pomp and circumstance for Mom's benefit, saying I do and becoming husband and wife is all that matters, right?" He brought my hand to his lips for a kiss and my heart squeezed over his use of the word wife.

"You're right. I just think I'd be more comfortable if you'd given me a budget. Like, *'Here's ten thousand dollars. Make our day special.'*"

He snorted and scratched the back of his head. "Add a couple of zeros to that, sweetness."

My eyes bulged out of their sockets so hard I thought they'd bleed. He chuckled and leaned in, brushing my favorite spot under my earlobe with his lips.

"Don't look so scared. It won't be hard to spend it all once things start adding up. You'll see." He finished the last bites of sandwich and scone and stood. "Let's go meet up with Mom. I can't wait to see the ballroom where I get to dance the night away at our reception with my wife in my arms."

Rex's face glowed as much as a man's could right now, and I never wanted to see that light dim. But I still worried. Our romance happened so fast, and had been a lot to absorb, and with less than a year to plan a fancy wedding—I hoped I wouldn't disappoint him. Or his mother.

**WHAT TO READ NEXT: Bonus novella—Chelsea and Rex get married in It Happened One Christmas Wedding,** free to read in KU.

# ZEEIRWINAUTHOR.COM

**If you love steamy small town romance with billionaires, military guys, hot hockey players or cowboys, then you've come to the right author! :)**

Check out all of my books at:
ZeeIrwinAuthor.com/series

You can also join my reader groups on Facebook to interact with me about my books and more at:

The Kissing Springs Reader Group.

# THE FATED LOVES SERIES

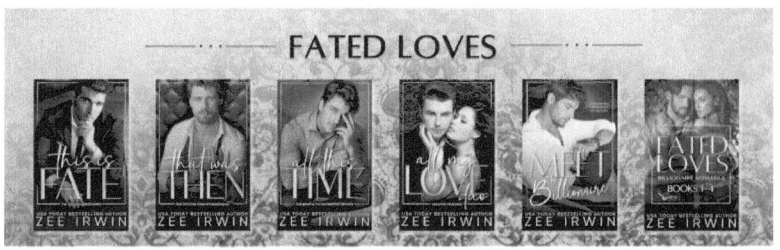

Rich men from Boston, each possessively loyal, work to protect the women they love.

# STEELE VALLEY BILLIONAIRES SERIES

In this new spinoff from Zee Irwin's Fated Loves Series, come billionaires who spend and love with reckless abandon while enjoying getaways to a small town mountain resort built for the rich and famous. Only there's nothing small about Steele Valley. Hearts love deeper, the bedroom windows get steamier, and stakes are higher.

# KISSING SPRINGS

## STEAMY SMALL TOWN SWOON COLLECTION

# THE LOVE BEACH FOREVER SERIES

Enjoy three connected steamy romances set in the small beach town of Love Beach, South Carolina, each with a hint of mystery and suspense.

# THE OFF-DUTY RESCUE RANCH

Three steamy, small town military romances provide the holiday origin story for the Off-Duty Rescue Ranch. If you love hot former military men, strong women, and matchmaking horses, then start reading today. Books 1-3 complete. More books from a new ranch coming soon.

Read *Return to Glendale Falls*, and join the Hale family sisters as they navigate life, love, and triumph in the face of loss. A free series with a new book added each year for subscribers to Zee's VIPs newsletter.

# ALSO BY ZEE IRWIN

**For a complete list of Zee Irwin's books, go to
ZeeIrwinAuthor.com/series**

## <u>Steamy Small Town Series:</u>

Kissing Springs Steamy Small Town Swoon Collection

Off-Duty Rescue Ranch Series

Love Beach Forever Series

Return to Glendale Falls Series

Love and Thorns Series

The Good Sons Series (coming 2026)

## <u>Hot Hockey players:</u>

The Hockey USA Collection

The Puckers: Steamy Hockey Romance Series

## <u>Billionaires/Wealthy CEOs:</u>

The Fated Loves Series (Boston)

Steele Valley Billionaires Series (Small Town)

It Happened Series (New York City and Small Town)

View Zee's audiobooks here.

# ABOUT THE AUTHOR

## ZEE IRWIN

Hello from Zee!

I'm a USA Today Bestselling Author, a bit of sunshine living in the countryside of Pennsylvania with my own grumpy alpha guy, two teenagers, and twin kitties. My favorite characters to write are small town heroes, hot hockey hunks, and growly ex-military mountain men, especially those who fall first, and are possessive of the women they love.

Keep up with me at ZeeIrwinAuthor.com for all my latest news.

facebook.com/zeeirwinromance
instagram.com/authorzeeirwin
amazon.com/author/zeeirwinromance
bookbub.com/profile/zee-irwin
goodreads.com/zee_irwin